FUELED DESIRE

J. MORGAN

ISBN-13: 978-0-9913482-7-5

Edited by Rebecca Cartee

Edited by Chelly Hoyle Peeler

❀ Created with Vellum

WHAT READERS ARE SAYING ABOUT THE SOUTHERN ROOTS SERIES!

MUST READ!!!!!! Seriously......MUST READ!!!!!!!!!!!! One Click RIGHT NOW! – Amazon review

Holy hotness batman! – Engaging Secrets Publishing

A captivating contemporary romance!! One you don't want to miss!!! – Crazy Chix Book Reviews

Rock and Roll hit! – Amazon review

Funny, hot... kilted... with heart. Need I say more? An AMAZING series! – TnA O'Malley

True romance story, beautifully written. – Amazon review

ACKNOWLEDGMENTS

My amazing BETA TEAM! Thank you so much for everything! I'm so glad Clive was so well received... with whipped cream on top of course!

Rebecca – Thank you for your mad editing skills and the commentary.

Chelly – You ROCKED! Thank you so much for coming in last minute and working your magic!

My family and friends that have supported me through this endeavor. Thank you for everything you do.

To my husband John – Thank you for the many nights away and listening to me when I needed to run ideas by you, even the laughs we shared. I love you to the moon and back.

For Heather and Amanda...

*S*eeing Lexi on the television next to her Senator husband was too much for me. That should have been me up there on his arm... the Senator's wife, not her. The farmer's daughter life is what Lexi had. I grew up with wealth and a damn silver spoon. What do I have to show for it? Nothing. Does anyone care? Hardly.

Every fucking day Mama makes a point to tell me how disappointed she is in me. Some days I wonder if she is actually talking about me... or possibly herself.

She's been drunk almost every night since I was about twelve. If my father had not made the investments he did and made the money that soon came after, I often wonder if he would have been home more. I wonder if this would have made a difference with Mama, or even our relationship.

I sighed and lay back on my bed. I stared at my ceiling for a while as thoughts ran through my mind.

Traveling the world.

Scotland.

India.

Australia.

All the different places I have always wanted to see, but never took the time. I've been so busy with my own life, trying to please Mama, trying to be the good daughter, that I never took any time for me. The real me; the me that was trapped inside, dying to get out. It never changed.

Hell, even when I was fucking Blaine behind Lexi's back, I never considered how this would make her feel. Blaine was mine. Well, at least in my mind he was… until the night he demanded I tell Robert he was fucking Lexi in the bathroom and not me. That moment clarified exactly what I was doing.

I closed my eyes and a tear slipped into my hair. As I wiped it off, the words slut, tramp, and whore ran through my mind. I often heard these from Mama and I sometimes heard people whisper it behind my back. I always thought they were jealous…

Well, no more will I be slut, tramp, and whore. As of today, as of right now, I'm the new Abby Masters. I refuse to be anything else. I refuse to be used and abused any longer.

Oh, poor little rich girl. I snorted at the thought. "Yeah, fuck you society and what you think of me." I flipped off the then sat up. I had enough money saved that I could back pack across Europe if I wanted. Then again, my version of back packing is staying in a Hilton. I shook my head and made my way into my closet.

The light flicked on as I walked inside. My clothes from different designers, some of them worn once, some with price tags still on them, stared at me. I touched a few of the garments and wondered why I had wanted these so badly when I bought them.

"Probably because someone else eyed them. Heaven forbid someone have something I don't." Where the hell did I go wrong? When did I become this person? I sighed and shoved at my designer tops. A suitcase sat in wait in the back of my closet. If it had been a beacon, it would have lit up. I grabbed it and opened it up. I could relate to the emptiness inside. No contents… like my heart.

"Fuck this shit. I'm changing and I'm outta this fuckhole town."

~

"What do you mean you're leaving?" Mama was slightly buzzed. It was two in the afternoon. I think I was a little disappointed, she's usually three sheets to the wind by now.

"Just what I said, Mama. I'm leaving. I want to explore the world and I can't do it living here."

She laughed and shook her head. "What, honey, did you fuck all the men in town and need fresh meat?"

To say I was shocked at her words doesn't begin to cover how I felt. She's my mother, yet, for some reason, she absolutely hates me.

"Oh don't be so shocked, child." She patted my face with a smirk. "I'm sure you'll have some idiot under your spell very soon. That's one asset your father gave you." She snorted and turned her back to me.

I had half a mind to throw something at her. The vase in the den was looking pretty good. "Well, I can see I'll be missed here," I said to her sarcastically. I squeezed my eyes to keep the tears from giving me away. I would not give her the satisfaction of crying. She had taken too many tears from me already. "Good bye, Mama. I'll tell Daddy I left. Coming from you, you might make it sound like you forced me to leave."

"Whatever," she mumbled, then she tripped. The wall caught her fall and she left an indention in the molding. Maybe she's a little more drunk than I thought. "Good God, child, get the fuck out of my house before you force me to kick your ass out!" Her voice rose in a scream.

I quickly turned away and left the den. My hands were wiping my cheeks as I made my way to the front door. My suitcase was packed with a few days' worth of clothes. Anything else I would need, I would pick it up on the way.

Good thing Daddy put my car in my name. Mama would probably call the police and tell them that it was stolen.

As I made my way outside and closed the door behind me, I suddenly couldn't breathe. I sucked in air but it wasn't making its way into my lungs. I felt like I was drowning. I coughed hard and bent over, then caught myself on my suitcase.

"Ms. Abby, are you okay, Ms. Abby?" Scott, our gardener was suddenly at my side. His hand touched my back and he bent over to look at my face.

I turned and glanced in his direction and at his words, are you okay, I realized... I was. I nodded a few times then finally, took in a deep breath.

"Yes, Scott, thank you. For once, I think I'm okay. No wait, I know I'm okay." I smiled and wondered if I were having some kind of panic attack. I've never been on my own, aside from my dorm in college. Not that *that* counts, of course.

"May I get you some water, Ms. Abby?" Scott was a nice man. My family didn't deserve someone nice. They didn't deserve much of anything. I know I certainly didn't.

I shook my head. "No, thank you, Scott. I'm good." I smiled and wondered if before now, had I ever had a conversation with Scott? Probably not. Being stuck in my own world of Abby Masters didn't leave much room for anyone else.

"Scott, are you happy here? Because if you're not, please, just fucking quit."

His brows rose in surprise... maybe shock. Scott shook his head. "I suppose you could consider me happy. I am paid to keep your garden."

"Oh Scott, it's not my garden you keep. It's my mother's."

Scott appeared to have blushed. It is hot here in Texas, but a few minutes ago, his face had not been flushed. My brow rose. "Scott, be careful with my mother. She's not who she seems to be."

"Ahh, your mother is fine, Ms. Abby." It was at this moment that Scott realized my suitcase was at my side. "Ms. Abby, are you going on a trip?"

I nodded and lowered my gaze. "Something like that. Scott?" I glanced up to find the gardener watching me. "Leave here and find something new. She doesn't deserve your kindness." Scott's mouth opened to say something but I stopped him. I held my hand up and shook my head. "Don't, just please, help yourself and leave. The moment she realizes she has no further need for you, she'll toss you away just like she did to me."

Pressing the key lock, the doors to my Audi unlocked. I opened the trunk and Scott was nice enough to lift my bag inside.

"Ms. Abby, please, don't leave like this. Your mother loves you."

I laughed and glanced at the gardener. "She has no idea what love is and it's obvious neither do you. Good day, Scott, and thank you for my bag." I closed the trunk then climbed into the front seat, closing the driver's door. I pressed the button to turn on the car and it began to purr. I glanced over at Scott, who was wearing the saddest face I've ever seen on a man. It was almost pathetic.

Leaving my home wasn't as hard as I thought it would be. My stomach was in knots though. I wasn't sure if it was from the almost panic attack or the conversation I was about to have with my father. I sighed heavily, knowing it was definitely the latter.

After twenty minutes of driving toward downtown Fort Worth, I pulled into my father's firm and stared at the building. He was the man in charge and most days, he was here. Today, I wondered if he was working, if he was still with his secretary, or if he'd finally given up on her.

My phone in hand, I pressed the speed dial to his private line. It rang twice and he answered.

"Phil Masters."

"Daddy?" I barely whispered then cleared my throat. "Daddy?" My stomach was hurting in a pretty bad way and my chest tightened.

"Abby? Is everything all right?" There was a slight alarm in his voice. I wondered if Mama called him.

"Yes, I'm fine. I called," I swallowed hard, "to tell you I'm leaving."

"Oh, all right, darling. Let us know when you get there, okay? I'm a little busy right now." I heard a faint giggle in the background. I sighed and knew he had no idea what I was doing.

"I'm not coming back." I waited for his response. I wondered if he had even heard me. I was about to speak again when he finally spoke something.

"Right. I'm sure I'll see you at dinner tonight. Don't be reckless, Abby. It would kill your mother." Then… he hung up.

Once again, a tear streamed down my cheek. I threw my phone across my car and screamed. My mother hates me and my father doesn't even know I exist. Right. Yes. Everything is about to completely change. Starting right now.

2

I laid my bank card and passport on the desk of the travel agent at the airport. The woman looked a little rough around the edges, so to speak. She was a little heavy set and a paper bag from McDonald's sat beside her. She tapped her chipped nails on the keyboard a few times. Her dark brown eyes met mine and she breathed heavily to brush the grayed hair from her eyes.

"Well, looks like I have a first class ticket to Scotland and a few coach seats." She glanced at my passport and the screen again. "Umm… Ms. Masters? Does your father know you're leaving the country?"

I was a little shocked at this question. "I didn't realize it was customary for the travel agents to ask such questions. Not that it is your business, but yes, he knows."

"Actually, it kind of is my business. He's an important man with a lot of power. We see him on the television almost daily. In this position, the power comes with perks." She tried to smile, maybe in an attempt to backpedal her earlier accusation.

I sighed and leaned forward. "Listen," I glanced at her name-plate, "Maggie. I'm planning a trip to Scotland, then to India, and eventually, Australia. He knows of my affairs and has already approved them. If you need to make a call, I'll be happy to dial the number." I smiled and tilted my head. I kept my eyes locked on hers, something my father taught me many years ago.

If you want to win an argument, if you want to win the sale, you will ask your question and be silent until they answer. Whoever speaks first or looks away loses.

Maggie fussed in her seat for a moment and immediately shifted her gaze.

I win.

"Well, Ms. Masters, since he knows about it, I guess that's okay. You are an adult, after all."

I kept my gaze hard on hers. My brow lifted as if to challenge her.

"Right," she began and looked to her computer again. "Looks like I can have you in Scotland as early as tomorrow. The flight leaves in a few hours. It is on to India the next week and then your final destination, Australia. When do you require a return flight?" She glanced at me with a smile.

"I don't need one."

Her eyes widened. "What?"

I shook my head. "What I meant was, I don't need one right away. I can book that later, right?"

Maggie nodded. "Of course." She grabbed for whatever beverage was in her McDonald's paper cup and she took a long pull. The brown liquid invaded her mouth and I could only imagine it was Diet Coke.

"Good. Then please set it up." I slid my bank card a little closer to her. Maggie picked it up and watched me for a moment, then turned to her computer. She keyed in a few more options then printed out my itinerary. She then swept my card through her reader. A few sounds transpired as the charge took place. Maggie finally handed my card back, along with my airline tickets and itinerary.

"Ms. Masters, I do hope you have a good flight. And be safe. Scotland is beautiful this time of year. India, well I don't know much about India but I've heard the air quality is not as good as it is here. Oh! And Australia! I've always wanted to go!" Maggie's eyes lit up in wonder at her own daydreams.

"Well, I'll be sure to send a post card." I stood and grabbed my suitcase. "Thank you, Maggie. You've been a great help today." I turned my back to her to leave when she spoke up.

"Would you really send me a post card?"

I glanced over my shoulder to the woman. Her eyes were doe with want... maybe acceptance. I can remember all the times I would look at my mother this way. Old Abby would laugh and tell her fat chance. I simply smiled and offered a nod. "Of course." Maggie grinned ear to ear.

I made my way toward security. Having already checked my bag, I sat my purse, shoes, and laptop on the conveyor. I stepped through and waited. The bags came through and the security guard made a mark on my ticket.

"Have a nice flight, Ms. Masters." A tall, slender black man nodded at me. I assumed he had no idea who I was or I would have been personally escorted to my gate. I had to say, this was kind of nice.

"Thank you." I smiled and took my ticket. I pulled my shoes back on, then grabbed my purse and laptop. Another security guard stepped around and watched me for a moment, then whispered something to the man who had handed me my ticket.

They looked at one another then at me. This was my cue to continue walking on as if I were clueless. Thinking I was in the clear, I felt a tap on my shoulder.

I turned to find the slender man who had handed me my ticket behind me. I glanced at his badge, his name was Dwayne.

"Ms. Masters, may I walk you to your designated gate? I do apologize in advance, but you are so much more attractive in person than on the television."

I smiled and shook my head. "It's okay, Dwayne." He nodded to confirm that was his name. "It was actually kind of nice to not be known." Dwayne smiled and offered to take my laptop. I shook my head and pulled it over my shoulder. It was almost awkward to be hit on, without being hit on.

"Where are you headed?" he asked me.

"Scotland, India, and then finally, Australia."

"Oh wow, now that is a vacation!" Dwayne chuckled. "I hope someday to get up to North Dakota. That's where my family is from. At least that's what I'm told."

"Well, Dwayne, I hope you make it up that way as well. Go a little farther north and you could venture into Canada." I smiled and he nodded.

"Here we are. Is there anything else, Ms. Masters?" Dwayne watched me for a moment and I shook my head.

"No, thank you. I'm good."

"Yes, ma'am. All right then, have a good flight." Dwayne nodded at me, then turned and walked back toward the security station. Nice guy and it was a pleasant conversation, one I don't get to have too often.

~

I found my seat in first class and relaxed. After a while, the flight attendant handed me a diet coke and shooter of spiced rum. All I needed now was a valium. This would be a long flight and I would rather sleep through it than not.

A young man with the reddest hair I have ever seen sat down next to me. I could not stop looking at him. He glanced over and furrowed his brows, then looked away. He had on a blue polo shirt and a black kilt. I've never seen a man in a kilt before, other than on television. It was... different. I couldn't see his legs too well as the end of it covered him to his knees.

"I'm sorry," I told him in a soft voice, "but I've never seen hair as red as yours! Is it natural?" Oh my God, did I really just ask him that?

Thank goodness he smiled. The man looked back over to me and his green eyes lit up in humor. He smiled and it was pleasant. He said something I did not recognize immediately. It was definitely English, but there was no deciphering it.

I blinked. He chuckled.

"Aye, let me try that once more."

I grinned and nodded.

"Never has anyone asked me such things as that, lass."

"Lass? Did you seriously just call me lass? Wow…" I shook my head. "Stereotype much?"

"I could ask ye the same thing," he retorted.

"Touché." This would either be a fun flight or the longest, most boring day and night in my life. If this conversation turned south, I would definitely need a valium.

The man with the red hair and bright green eyes chuckled. "The name's Clive. Where ye be headed, ma dear?"

I grinned and shook my head. "Clive, who is obviously not from Texas, I'm headed to Scotland. I'll venture to guess you're headed home?"

"What gave it away? Ma accent or the red hair?" He chuckled and waved down the flight attendant. As she approached, Clive tapped his chin for a moment. "I don't imagine ye have any Irish whiskey on board?"

The flight attendant shook her head then glanced at me. I smiled and she returned it.

"Right. Probably no whipped cream either?"

Now I'm curious. "Clive?" He looked over at me and raised his brows. "Whipped cream?"

"Aye, ma darling. Good with the coffee. Well, that is if they had Irish whiskey." He looked back to the attendant. "How about some tea then, aye? Ye can do tea?"

"Yes, sir, I certainly can." She smiled and made her way back to the preparation area.

I smirked and watched Clive for a moment. "Strong morning drinks?"

Clive chuckled and shook his head. "I do happen to thoroughly enjoy ma Irish coffee, thank ye very much. However," he leaned in and lowered his voice, "I'm Scottish, not Irish. I may be wearing ma kilt in the traditional style. Care to check?" He waggled his brows.

Oh, I believe I will actually enjoy this flight very much. If this conversation continues with Clive, I don't imagine I'll be sleeping much. Between the whipped cream, the possibility of his traditional kilt, then this accent of his… well, he's just too much fun to sleep through.

"I'll take your word for it." I felt my skin turn hot from the blush that rushed to my cheeks.

The flight attendant came back with hot water and a Lipton tea bag. I think Clive would have choked if he had been sipping on the water.

"What the hell am I supposed to do with this?" he almost yelled.

The flight attendant's mouth opened and I think she was in shock.

"Clive," I began. He turned to face me and smiled. "The hot water is to steep the tea."

"Oh, I knew that, dear; I only wanted to get to her, make her squirm." He winked at me.

The flight attendant cleared her throat.

"Well, I think you have accomplished said squirming." I motioned to her and his eyes widened slightly. He turned to face her.

"Ahh right, well fetch me a few cubes of sugar, if ye would, then we'll call it even for not having any cream, whipped or otherwise." He pointed at me with his thumb. "The whipped stuff was for her anyway. She likes to lick it off me."

I gasped and the flight attendant laughed then covered her mouth. "That's so not true!" I announced. "I just met you!"

"All the better for the excitement!" Clive chuckled. "Ahh, ma dear, I'm only joshing with ye. Don't look at me like that. Ye look a bit stopped up."

I shook my head. "You're insane!"

He winked again. "Just wait till we land in Scotland, miss. Ye have seen nothing yet!"

3

Occasionally, I would glance over at Clive. He had begun to manhandle his iPod. He touched the screen and adjusted the volume on the side, then he sighed with a slight growl. It was a little sexy, I'll admit. I grinned at his torment. He deserved this after the scene he'd started earlier. Whipped cream? Right.

I glanced over again as he shoved the earbuds in his ears. He tapped them a few times then messed with the plug.

"Absolute piece of shit," he mumbled.

I knew I would regret this, "What's the problem?"

He glanced over at me then back at his iPod. "Piece of shit player won't play. I don't know what the hell it wants from me."

"Just your patience and understanding, Clive." I reached over and took his iPod. "One must love their object of affection if said objects are to work for them." I pressed the round button at the bottom for the main menu then pulled up the settings.

"Ahh, I see. So if I treat ye right, ye will love me tonight, darling?"

I glanced over at him with mock terror on my face. He laughed a hard, belly laugh. A few of the passengers glanced over at us.

"You will keep your voice down, damn you!" I scolded. "I'm trying to help you here!"

"Mmm, aye, I'll let ye help me darling, that's for sure." He wiggled his brows at me. I just shook my head.

"Keep that shit up you'll get yourself a black fucking eye. You understand?" I pointed my finger at him. Clive smirked.

"Don't get the panties in a bundle, doll. I'm only joshing with ye. Besides, if ye get ma blasted headphones to work, I'll leave ye alone."

I considered this for a moment and sighed. As much as I wanted him to stop talking, a part of me was enjoying his company. Truth be told, he was making me laugh, if anything, on the inside. It had been a very long time since I'd had a male friend. Not that I was counting on Clive to be this person but his entertainment was enjoyment enough; even if it was for just this flight.

"If I get this to work for you, you promise to stop having fits on the plane like you're a demented patient that has escaped from the hospital?"

He grinned. "Who told ye about me?"

I laughed; I couldn't help it. "Oh Clive, you're too much."

"That's what she said last night." He chuckled. I shook my head.

Seeing his settings were fine, I pushed in the headphones a little more until I felt a click. I smirked and handed it over.

"Fixed," I said and waited.

He placed the earbuds in his ears and pressed play... then jumped. "Fuck me!" He quickly turned it down as the neighboring passenger hissed.

"Keep it down!" The woman shook her head. Her short, pixie cut hair looked like it had been styled before she'd left for the airport. Now it was mashed to the back of her head. She rolled her eyes and her long, fake lashes made the effort even more dramatic. Clive noticed it, too.

"Ma apologies, ma lady. We didn't mean to offend the elderly."

The pixie cut woman gasped and glared at Clive. The woman couldn't have been older than twenty-three.

"I'll have you know I'm NOT elderly!"

Clive shrugged then turned his attention back to me.

"You're relentless, you know that?" I tried to cover the smile that threatened to express the amusement I was feeling.

He smirked. "I enjoy making people laugh. I'm a bartender by day, psychoanalyst by night." He leaned in and lowered his voice. "Ye are talking to ma secret identity."

I giggled; I couldn't help it. "Well, secret identity, umm," I considered a witty comeback but was afraid I would fall short on this one. "I don't have a secret identity." I suddenly felt like I was lying. I did have a secret; it wasn't something I was proud of. I'd fucked my best friend's boyfriend. I'd taken random men home and had sex with them. Hell, my mother might have been right; I was a whore.

My smile faltered and I turned away from Clive to stare out the window. The skyline had turned to darkness so there wasn't much to stare at, other than my own reflection in the thick glass.

He tapped my shoulder but I refused to look at him.

"Let me tell ye something; I know exactly who ye are."

I closed my eyes and sighed. "You know nothing about me."

"I know ye enjoy a good sense of humor. I know ye are taking a trip away from whatever is here because it is obvious ye are miserable."

I turned my gaze to him and met his eyes. I didn't know what to say, so I continued to listen.

"There's a woman inside you, dying to get out." Clive grinned and leaned in slightly. "If ye will allow me, I'll be happy to help get her out."

"How?" I mumbled to him.

He looked up the aisle, then back down. He grinned and turned back to me. "Meet me in the bathroom in five minutes." He winked.

I blinked, having no idea what to say to this. At first, I thought he was truly reading me, understanding me. Hell no, he's full of shit. I shook my head and turned back to my window.

"Ahh c'mon, darling, I'm only teasing with ye."

I felt his arm touch my own and I sighed again. "Clive, just…"

"No, now ye listen."

I raised a single brow and turned back to face him. "Excuse me?"

"I told ye: bartender psychoanalyzer. I read people better than they read themselves. I can tell ye are running from something, but I have no idea what. Most likely, the life ye have here in bum fuck Texas. Tell me I'm close."

I lowered my gaze and nodded. "Too close."

"Good. Then tell ye what. Once we land, I'll give ye the name of ma bar. Come see me and drinks are on the house. Ye can tell me what ye are running away from and I'll continue to get ye bloody drunk until ye agree to fuck me."

"Oh my god, what?" I quickly turned to him with widened eyes. I couldn't believe he'd actually just said that to me.

"Ahh gotcha, didn't I? Just making sure ye are paying attention. Oh, but by all means, the whipped cream is on the table." He winked. "Always will be." He grinned and placed his earbuds in and pressed play again. He adjusted the volume on his player and relaxed in his seat.

Who the hell was sitting next to me? Who the hell was this man? I continued to stare at him until he opened his eyes. He smiled and winked at me again. I felt the heat rise in my cheeks and it wasn't from blushing. This man, this stranger, was making me angry.

He thinks he knows me. He thinks he can judge me by my actions. He thinks I'll put out if I'm drunk enough.

Hell girl, you would. Why deny it?

Fuck you, inner voice. Fuck you.

~

*a*t some point, I fell asleep. Clive finally left me alone, at least long enough to sleep. I was jolted awake between the flight attendant preparing us for landing, the plane hitting a bit of turbulence and... of course, Clive trying to peek down my blouse.

His hand was reaching to adjust my top when I slapped it away and sat up in my seat. "Seriously? Who the fuck does that?"

He winked. "Good morning, beautiful. Need coffee? You're a righteous bitch in the morning, aren't ye?" He chuckled and waved for an attendant.

I growled. "You were checking out my goods while I was sleeping! Of course I'm a bitch in the morning!"

"Nah love, ye just need a good fucking in the morning to wake up, that's all." He looked at me and smiled. "Ye need a good fucking?"

"Oh my GOD, stop talking!" I ran my hands through my hair and looked out the window at the beautiful greenery that had come into view.

"You need a good fucking in the morning to wake you up," I mumbled to myself. "To a perfect stranger. Who does that?" I shook my head and found myself smiling. Then the smiling turned into a giggle. I slowly turned back toward Clive and all he had to do was wiggle his brows. That's when I knew I had lost all sense. I busted out laughing and covered my mouth.

Pixie cut was glaring at us and shook her head.

"Oh get stuffed," I yelled out. Clive's brows shot up and Pixie cut's mouth dropped open in surprise.

"Look, Clive," I started. "She's inviting you over. Her mouth is open and ready." I winked. Pixie cut's face turned red. Clive barked out a laugh so loud, a few of the other passengers turned to see what was so funny.

"Oh doll, we're going to get along just fine."

For some reason I knew he was right. I also felt like I was about to get into a lot of trouble... much needed trouble.

Pixie cut stood and quickly grabbed her bags, then headed down the aisle. She said something to the flight attendant who glanced our way. She was the same one Clive had teased last night. When Pixie cut turned away, the attendant shook her head and smiled in our direction.

Clive chuckled and leaned over to me. "Shall we pick this up at baggage claim?"

"Only if you have breakfast with me. This righteous bitch needs her coffee."

He chuckled. "Deal."

A few minutes had passed before Clive finally stood. He looked down at me and winked. He reached above his head and opened the overhead compartment. When he reached up, his blue polo pulled up just enough to show a serious six-pack of abs underneath his shirt.

He pulled his bag down and it was at that moment, I saw his arms. I suppose sitting next to me I didn't get the full extent of what his size was. Clive was tall, thickly strong, and holy shit, was he beautifully handsome.

Shit, Abby, don't do this, not with a man you just met.

No, it won't be like that. We'll be friendly then when he gives me his number, I'll throw it away.

No, you won't.

I hate this inner voice of mine. It gives me a fucking headache.

"Are ye ready, doll?" He smiled down at me and pulled me from my inner argument. I nodded and stood. My legs felt sore from sitting and lying back most of the night.

I ran my fingers through my long blond hair then pulled a clip from my purse. I pulled it up in a messy twist and clipped it. I felt a few strands of hair fall into my face. Clive must have noticed it as well, if the intense stare he was giving me was any indication.

Once I stepped out into the aisle, I cleared my throat. "I, umm, need my bag."

"Oh right!" He reached up and pulled it out for me. His arms flexed and I felt my mouth water. What the fuck was wrong with me?

We made it off the plane and headed toward baggage claim. The train ride over was silent between us. I found this odd, having just met the man; he was a talker. Now he chose this time to be quiet.

I glanced around the train car and did some people watching. Couples were talking to their children. Lovers were embracing one another, whispering something that would make the other blush. I found myself watching them for a moment... that is until I felt Clive's breath against my neck. I flinched slightly as he spoke.

"Would ye like me to whisper sweet things in ye ear, doll? Because I can. I'll even lick ye ear for effect."

I leaned away from him then looked his direction. "You have to be kidding me." He shook his head. I smiled and tried not to laugh. At the same time, I felt the heat between my thighs ignite. I wanted to find out if he really did wear his kilt in the traditional style. I wanted to find out more about Clive. I didn't know this man but it was obvious my body wanted to know him. Hell, he was sexy. Who wouldn't?

If I had met him in a bar here in Scotland, would I have gone home with him? Hell yeah, I would have. Would it have been the right decision during my life changing, Abby-needs-to-find-herself mission? Fuck no.

"One step at a time, Clive. Bags first, then coffee. If you're still hanging around, then we'll talk about your bar. Sound like a deal?"

He grinned and nodded. "Sure, doll. Now," he leaned in and lowered his voice. "Do ye like yer coffee strong or weak? Because out here, the coffee is very strong. Keeps ye up for hours into the wee morning." He winked.

I wanted to giggle at the mention of wee morning, but decided against it. "Why do I feel there's an ulterior motive to your coffee inquiry?"

He chuckled. "Ahh love, only joshing with ye." He sat back and relaxed in the car, then stretched his arms across the backside. His legs sat apart and if I were across the car, I'm positive I would have been given the full view. He had to have on underwear... at least I hoped he did.

I glanced over to the romantic couple in their embrace. They would be oblivious. I looked to the family next to him. The children were playing around and the mother was keeping them together. She glanced over toward him and she smiled. He winked at her. She didn't take notice of anything obvious.

"So I'll take it you don't wear it traditionally?" I asked... boldly.

"Hmm?" He glanced over. "What, ma kilt? Woman, there are children present." He furrowed his brows at me. I shook my head and rolled my eyes at about the time the train came to a stop.

"Whatever, Clive," I began. "You talk a big game but when it comes down to it, that's it, just all talk." I grinned and mumbled to myself, "Pussy."

Clive suddenly stood and towered over me. The man was huge! The look in his eyes was intense. I couldn't help running my eyes down his body, then back up again. He raised a single brow then reached for my hand. I hesitantly put my hand in his. As I stood, he leaned in and whispered, "Pussy is what a man eats, not what a man is. Big difference, love."

I felt myself shiver. I hadn't realized he actually heard me. The doors opened but I couldn't move. My lips parted and I watched him for a moment. He chuckled, breaking the moment. "C'mon, love. Let's get ye bags and coffee."

I felt myself nod and swallowed hard. I needed to distance myself from this man... this hot, strong male in a black kilt who smelled so good. Fuck me. Clive was a Scot coming home from whatever visit to Texas he had taken. If I decided to hang out with Clive, I knew I would be in a heap of trouble.

India and Australia were still on my plate. I suddenly hoped like hell my trip to Scotland would hurry up and finish. The faster it went, the faster I would be away from Clive… and temptation.

"Where are ye staying, love?" His voice suddenly interrupted my thoughts. Where was I staying? I had made reservations but my mind… I can't think. I looked away from Clive and focused on the conveyor that was sending bags around in circles. I saw my Louis Vuitton coming my way. I had bought the luggage not too long ago. I had clipped a large red baggage tag to it so I knew this was definitely mine.

"I'm at the W hotel in downtown Turnberry." I glanced over at him and found him watching me. As the conveyor continued to move, my bag came closer. I broke eye contact with him, the intensity was becoming almost too much.

I bent over, grabbed my bag, and heaved. I don't remember it being this heavy. Then again, Clive's eyes on me was not helping that either.

"Allow me." He wrapped his large hand around mine and pulled. I quickly let go and pulled my hand away. He set it on the ground then stood straight. "Do ye have anything else?"

I shook my head. "No, this is it."

"Wow, ye are roughing it, aren't ye?" I glanced up at him and he smirked.

"I suppose, but I don't need much. I plan to travel, not dress up. I'm not here to…" I trailed off and lowered my gaze. "Clive, thank you for the wonderful travel conversation, but…"

"No buts. C'mon, I'll take ye to yer hotel."

"What?" I looked up and shook my head. "That's not necessary. I can manage."

"I have no doubt ye will manage just fine, woman, but I won't take no for an answer. Allow me to take ye. If it makes ye feel better, ye may jump from ma jeep once we arrive. I won't stop. Ye may roll to safety." He winked and gave me a smile that melted a part of me.

I giggled slightly then nodded. "As long as you let me roll on the grass, then sure, you may take me."

$\sim$

*T*urns out, I didn't have to roll after all. Clive pulled into the circular drive of the hotel. The bell staff came out and approached the driver's side door.

"Ahh, I'm not staying. The lady is exiting the car, not I."

I watched him for a moment. The side door opened as the bell staff waited.

"Madam?" I lowered my gaze from Clive then slid out of the Jeep.

"Thank you, Clive, for the ride." I lowered my head and looked at him through hooded lids. I knew this was one of my seduction techniques, but for Clive, it wasn't necessarily needed. I could see his response in his features. He liked it.

"Before ye get too far away, here." He leaned over and placed a card in my hand. When I glanced at it, the name, *Hitter's Bar*, was on the top of it and below that, *Clive Patterson, Owner*. I ran my thumb over the raised ink then lifted my gaze to his.

"Nice to officially meet you, Clive Patterson."

He nodded. "May I call on ye?"

"I'm not sure how. My cell will not work out here." He gave an almost disappointed look. "But I tell you what. You know where I'm staying and I know where you work. I'm sure we'll be bound to meet up somewhere."

Appearing satisfied, Clive nodded. "Ye bet yer sweet arse." He winked and I grinned.

"I'll see you later then, Clive of Hitter's Bar."

"And I'll see ye... hell, ye didn't give me yer name!"

I grinned and backed away from his Jeep. "That's because I

never gave it." I winked this time and turned to head toward the hotel.

"Ye are killing me, woman!" he yelled after me. "KILLING ME! And ye still owe me that coffee!" He held his hand over his heart as if to suggest heart failure. I grinned and walked inside the hotel.

4

he door to my suite closed behind me and I leaned against it. Clive was a very intense person and a lot to take in. If everyone in Scotland was like him, I was in big trouble. I can handle intense in small doses. Hell, I'm an intense person. But Clive? He's a lot to handle and I would be lying if I didn't admit he was a lot of man.

I sighed and pushed away from the door. Making my way across the room, I opened the curtains then let out a soft gasp; the view was breathtaking. The view of Firth of Clyde was just outside my bedroom... along with the greenest landscape I had ever seen. The golf courses in Texas had nothing on the grass here.

A knock sounded at my door and for the briefest of moments, I wondered if it was Clive. *That's ridiculous*, I told myself. I inhaled deeply, then slowly let it out as I crossed the room toward the door. I opened it and found the bell staff with my bags. The older gentleman stepped inside the room. He was tall and slender in his build, dark brown hair. His tag read 'Reggie'.

He laid my suitcase on my bed then sat my laptop bag on the accompanying desk. He turned toward me and smiled.

"Will there be anything else?"

I shook my head. "I haven't been through currency exchange yet. Would you accept American dollars as a tip?"

"A tip, madam?" He tilted his head, looking to me with a curious expression.

"Yes, a tip. Money paid for your services."

He smiled, but it appeared forced. "We do not accept... tips... madam. If there will be nothing else..." He waited and I shook my head. I felt like I had offended the man, but how would I have known? I had no idea what customs were here in Scotland.

"No, I'm good, thank you."

He lowered his head in a slight bow then walked past me. When the door closed suddenly, I jumped at the sound. We tended to complain a lot in the States about foreigners who failed to learn our language or learn our customs. Hell, I should have done the same. I'm an idiot.

My ears rang slightly from the silence. I'm alone, totally alone. I've never been alone. I've always had my parents around; whether I was home or in college... didn't matter, they were there. My friends were only a walk or drive away.

I did well at pushing everyone away from me.

I remembered when I told Lexi why I pushed people away. She had to have known I was fucking Blaine.

I keep people at arm's length. That way they can't get close enough to hurt me. I'm in control of my feelings, no one else.

Letting out a long sigh, I looked around my large suite, taking it all in. My bedroom sat unoccupied. A huge king sized bed just for me. The den had a couch and coffee table. The kitchenette was furnished with the supplies I had ordered online for my stay. I loved that about this hotel.

I smiled but it wasn't because I was happy to be here. I smiled because for once, I was actually on my own. I had heard it was liberating, although I wasn't quite sure I felt that yet.

Yet.

After I unpacked and hung up my garments, I called down to the front desk to inquire about transportation. Scheduled tour buses came and went throughout the day. Did I really want to tour? Yeah, I guess I did. It had been so long since I'd been to a museum outside of Fort Worth and Dallas.

I wonder what Clive is doing?

Stop it.

Call him. Talk dirty on the phone. He won't know it's you.

No. Clive will have to wait. Why the hell would I talk dirty?

I was here for an adventure, not sex games. I've left the old Abby behind. No more self-abuse. No more self-absorbance. No more... anything. New Abby. New me. New experiences. New everything.

I stepped into my bedroom and jumped across my bed. My body bounced a few times until I settled down. It was so comfortable. If I allowed myself, I could probably sleep for days. There was no one to tell me to get up. No one to tell me to look pretty for the cameras. No one to put me down.

It was this thought that caused me to think of my mother. She had no idea where I was, other than traveling. I told my father but I seriously doubt he was listening. His secretary was too busy doing lord knows what.

I shuddered and sat up. "The right thing to do would be to tell my mom I'm here." I glanced at my laptop case, the laptop still inside my bag. "But all she would do is complain that she has no one around. Well, no one except Scott, the gardener slash pool boy." I rolled my eyes and stood to make my way into the bathroom. I glanced at myself in the mirror and pulled the clip from my hair. After stretching for a moment, I yawned.

Looking around my bathroom, it was huge. The shower was a walk in that was not enclosed. It didn't need to be. It had two overhead shower heads with accompanying shower heads for the body. It was big enough for two people comfortably. Oh, I knew I would absolutely indulge in this shower… often.

I reached over and turned it on. The water began to pour out and it was like a small waterfall. I smiled and began removing my clothes. Towels were set up next to the shower so I stepped into the hot water.

"This is what heaven must be like," I said to no one. I sighed and stood still for so long, I could have probably fallen asleep standing there.

I laughed to myself and stretched my arms, then squealed. I could sing, I could dance, and I could slip and fall on my ass. Wouldn't matter, I was alone.

After showering for way too long… who cared, it was amazing, I dried off, wrapped my hair in another towel, and pulled on a set of silky pajamas. I went back to the bathroom and combed out my hair, then put nightly moisturizer on my skin.

Picking up the remote, I stared at the blank television for a few minutes.

"What the hell are the stations here?"

I sighed and turned on the television, then crawled into bed. I'm not sure if I was tired enough to go to sleep, but hell, I would definitely try. I slept plenty on the plane but I felt restless. I wasn't sure what to do first while I was here. Loch Ness? Museums? I yawned again then wiped the dampness from my eyes.

The television was set to what appeared to be a local news channel. I had no idea of the politics here, I knew Scotland had voted to have their own independence and lost. I cannot fathom how that would feel in the United States. I wondered if there was a Loch Ness Monster. Hell, I guess I could find out. I grinned to myself and snuggled into my bedding.

The pillow absorbed my head as the bed welcomed me to my new temporary home. It was quiet and amazing. I yawned again and felt my eyes become heavy. I knew I would have jet lag but I wasn't sure when it would hit. Maybe I was still too high on excitement to care.

I could be high on Clive right about now.

Stop it!

I sighed at my own thoughts and set the remote down. I felt my eyes begin to grow heavy. My lids began to drift closed as delicious thoughts of Clive entered my mind.

a knock at my door abruptly woke me from my sleep. I jumped in my bed and looked around. For a brief second, fear struck me. I forgot where I was and didn't recognize my surroundings, until it flooded back. My fear immediately shifted into excitement.

Freedom!

I pulled my silk robe around my body and made my way to the door. I glanced through the peephole and for a moment, I had wondered if Clive called me out on finding me here. I sighed in relief to find the bellman, Reggie, waiting on the other side. I also felt a little disappointed it wasn't Clive.

Just a little.

I opened the door just enough to look out. I smiled slightly and looked at Reggie. "Morning."

"More like afternoon, Miss. Fresh cart of coffee and tea at yer disposal." He stepped to the side and pulled a cart around.

I grinned and opened the door wider. "Afternoon? What time is it?"

Reggie pushed the cart inside my room then pulled his sleeve up to expose a black watch. "It would be fourteen thirty, Miss."

I gave him a blank expression and raised my brows. "Fourteen thirty?"

"Ahh," he grinned and intertwined his fingers behind his back. "I believe that would mean two thirty, Miss."

I pinched the bridge of my nose then rubbed my eyes. "Reggie," I glanced back to him, "do you happen to recall what time I arrived last night?"

"Ye did not arrive last night, Miss. Ye arrived morning before last."

"What?!" My eyes widened at this news. I slept for an entire day? Seriously? I looked at the balcony of my den and found the sky to be blue. How did I lose an entire day? "I must have been tired."

"Yes, Miss. Now if I may, I have provided the finest coffees and teas Scotland has to offer. If ye prefer something stronger, I'll be happy to send up different varieties of wine, liquor, and beer."

"Wine might be good later, Reggie. I feel... lost, I think."

"Probably jet lag, Miss."

I turned to face him. "Abby. Please, call me Abby." I smiled softly then turned away. "Reggie, where may I find information for tours of the city?"

"Downstairs at the information desk, M-Abby."

I smiled at him and he nodded.

"Will there be anything else?" He turned and headed toward the door.

"Just that wine later on, please."

"Ahh, yes. I'll have it sent up." He let himself out of the room.

I ran my hand through my hair and sat down on the couch. I had slept for an entire day. I don't recall ever doing that. Even as a child, my mother never allowed me to sleep longer than eight hours. Eventually, the eight became six, then five. Soon, I would be up all night with her as she drank herself unconscious. My father never knew most nights. He was never home.

I shook my head. "Whatever, time to get dressed, go out and explore!"

After cleaning up, fixing my hair, and getting dressed, I looked myself over in my mirror. I flat ironed my hair, pulled on a red fitted t-shirt and black shorts. Slipping on my red and black wedge sandals, I grabbed my purse and sunglasses. I took a deep breath and headed down to the information desk.

The woman behind the desk pointed me toward a rack of informational flyers. I scanned them over briefly, looking for something I have never experienced... other than Scotland.

"Blairquhan Castle. Interesting." I picked up the flyer and turned it over for information.

Blairquhan is a Regency era castle near Maybole in South Ayrshire, Scotland. It was the historic home of the Hunter-Blair Baronets and remained in the family's possession until 2012, when it was sold to a Chinese company.

"Hmm... sold or acquisitioned?" I thought aloud. The grounds appeared to be beautiful and it was open for tours. I held onto that one and pulled up another for the shopping district. Another flyer caught my eyes. Patterson Distillery. I picked it up and examined the cover. There was an image of a bottle of red wine pouring into a wine glass. The back panel had their location and reviews of the Distillery. "I enjoy wine, sounds fun."

I did a currency exchange with the front desk then headed out to find the hotel shuttle.

~

The tour of the castle was amazing. I have never been inside one, even when I was beginning my modeling adventure. I didn't want to think about that so I pulled out my next adventure. I pulled out my flyers and the first one I saw was the National Museum of Scotland.

A few of the cabs were lined up to take tourists wherever they wanted. My shuttle had since left so I opted for a new ride. The driver glanced over when I opened his door. He looked me over then turned on his fare light.

The man was older, pale, with grayish red hair. He smelled of smoke and I considered getting in another cab, until he put it into gear.

He spoke a language to me I did not understand. I felt unsure of what to do or say until he turned to look at me. "American?"

I nodded and smiled.

He nodded back then turned back to the street. "Where would ye like to go, Miss?" He pulled out onto the main street and looked in his rearview mirror at me.

"National Museum?"

"Sure thing." He pulled out in traffic and I relaxed in his back seat.

I thumbed through my other flyers and asked, "As a resident, umm," I glanced at his name, "Nick, where would you recommend someone new to visit?"

"What ye like, Miss?" He glanced at me and continued driving.

"Well, I have a flyer for the Patterson Distillery, this museum, and the shopping district."

"Ahh, all good places to frequent. Ye plan on seeing our Nessie?" He chuckled and glanced to me.

I smiled and shook my head. "Probably not. I'm not a believer."

"Well, that's too bad, then. Many people tend to have luck when they visit. Maybe if ye go, ye will have an adventure!" He grinned.

"Nick, I AM on an adventure. I'm from the States and I'm vacationing in Scotland." I grinned and placed my flyers in my purse.

"On holiday? Yeah, we have many travelers come about. Where else are ye headed to, Miss?"

"I have plans to explore India and eventually, Australia."

"Oh, I've never been outside Scotland. I hope ye enjoy it."

Nick pulled up to a curb and parked. "Here we are Miss, National Museum. Six euros, Miss." He held out his hand. I pulled out my wallet and pulled out what was required then handed it over.

"Nick, do you accept tips?"

"Tips, Miss?"

"Yes, extra funds for your services."

"Oh, well that is up to you, Miss, but normally, no."

"I guess that is an American thing, then."

Nick nodded and wished me farewell as I stepped out of his cab. I gasped at the sight of the museum. We had nothing like this in America. The circular portion of the building was taller and wider than the rest of the building combined. The outside windows were large and rectangular, upright. It was beautiful.

I pulled the door open and walked inside. Sharks and large fish hung from the ceiling while a large elephant greeted me at the front entrance. Ming, the Golden Empire looked interesting. I paid my entrance fee and began my tour through the museum.

I think I was maybe twenty minutes into looking around and found myself... bored. Museums are nice, but I think it is more fun if the experience is shared with someone.

Maybe the museum alone was not a good idea.

I sighed and made my way back toward the front. Shopping would be fun but I could do that any time. I pulled my sunglasses out and pushed them onto my face. My flyers fell to the floor. I squatted down to pick them up and Patterson Distillery was on top.

"Okay, Patterson Distillery, you're next."

I stood and shoved the flyers back into my purse, then made my way out front to hail a cab. To my pleasant surprise, Nick pulled up to the curb. I smiled.

When I opened the back passenger door, he glanced back. "Well, I thought I would hang out. I thought you might need a ride to yer next destination. Nessie?" he grinned.

I shook my head and closed the door. "Not today, Nick. Thank you. How about Patterson Distillery?"

"Ahh, good choice, Miss. The Patterson family has a legacy in place now. Great wine, great food, great people. All around, a great family, and fun to be with. I'm sure you'll have an excellent time."

"Oh, is the distillery a bar as well?"

"Something like that, Miss. You'll see."

Our destination took about half an hour to reach. We pulled into what appeared to be historic downtown Turnberry. At least, that is what the signs around me read.

"Eleven euros, Miss." Nick held out his hand as I placed the money into it.

"Will you hang around here for a few hours, Nick?" I grinned at his *are you kidding me* expression. "Can't blame a girl for asking."

He shook his head. "Afraid not. If you need a ride, give me a call." He handed over his business card. "I'll come pick you up."

"Thank you, Nick." I took the card and placed it in my purse. "You're very kind, thank you." I smiled and exited the car. "At least he wasn't short like Reggie," I told myself. Nick drove away as soon as I stepped onto the curb.

"Patterson Distillery" was in bright red lettering at the top of the big brown building in front of me. At the bottom, it read "Hitter's Bar".

I blinked and stared at it for a moment. I reached into my purse and pulled out my distillery flyer. Nothing on it read anything about Hitter's Bar.

Just to check, I pulled out Clive's business card he handed me night before last.

Hitter's Bar.

"Oh, you have to be kidding me," I said to myself. I looked at the bar again and the distillery lettering. "Is he Patterson Distillery? Oh, fuck my life."

I sighed and shoved the card and flyer back into my purse. I thought about using a phone... somewhere... to call Nick back to pick me up. I just got here. I didn't want to see Clive.

Did I?

Yeah, you do. You want to surprise him. You want to make him beg to know your name. You want to get drunk and you most definitely want to fuck him.

Stop it! Oh my god!

I shook my head and was tempted to smack myself for those thoughts. Clive was a very good-looking man, at least from what I remembered of him. I sighed and, against better judgment, I pulled open the door to Hitter's Bar.

6

*L*oud music filled the air, the smell of alcohol and men... real, unadulterated men. Some had on flannel kilts, others had on pants. I felt like I had walked onto a movie set. Good lord, there were a lot of men in this bar. Televisions lined the wall and played sports—from soccer to tennis to cricket. The bar was quite large. It was roomy and rustic looking.

A few of the men near the front stopped mid-sentence and looked my way. I stood out like a sore thumb. In America, I typically was the different one; tall and beautiful like... like a model. Here, I was different. I was average height, if not shorter. My light blonde hair was a contrast to the dark brown, auburn, and black shades that surrounded me. I swallowed hard and lowered my gaze, then walked farther inside the bar. The men inside were... hell, they were all tall! I'm tall for a female, standing at five foot ten. These men towered over me. What did they feed their children in Scotland? Good lord!

I found an empty table in one of the corners. It was in the shadows so I would be hidden. At least that is what I had hoped for.

I slid into the wooden chair and crossed my long legs. I placed my hands in my lap and looked around, taking it all in.

Pool tables, about four of them, were filled with players. Waitresses wearing black and white striped outfits, like referees, walked between the tables. A few pinball machines were set up and the bar was so long. There were so many taps, beers, and spouts.

And Clive.

"Oh, shit!" My eyes widened at the sight of him. He was laughing at something a patron had said. He shook his hand and nodded. Clive glanced at someone else and grabbed a tall glass that looked like a Guinness. When he put it under a tap, the black looking sludge that entered the glass proved my guess correct.

"May I get ye something, Miss?"

I glanced up at a brunette waitress whose arms were covered in tattoos, her face had at least five rings in it, and her smile... it was warm and welcoming.

"I hear you have a fine red wine I could sample?"

"Oh! American!" She grinned and pulled out the chair next to me and sat down. "Where are ye from, Miss, if I may ask?"

I smiled. "You may. I'm from Texas, one of the southern states."

"Ye sound like a cowboy!" She giggled. "Ma name is Scarlet. It is nice to meet ye, American girl!"

"It is nice to meet you, too, Scarlet. Now," I glanced over in Clive's direction. He hadn't seen me yet. Good. "How about that red wine?" I looked back at Scarlet and found her following my gaze.

"He's a hottie, isn't he?" Scarlet grinned and looked to me. "He's ma boss and all, but if he wasn't, I would totally snog him."

"Oh!" I laughed and shook my head. "Well, okay then."

Scarlet grinned. "I'm only saying he's hot!" she grinned. "Do ye know our Clive?"

"No, not really. We met once, but I didn't realize he owned this bar."

"Oh, he owns more than this bar, Miss. He owns Patterson Distillery. He owns the label, the wine, and the vineyard!"

I'm not sure how long I stared at Scarlet, but when she waved her hand in front of my face, I finally blinked. "I met him on the plane in Texas when he sat next to me. He's a... well, he's interesting."

"He's a fucker is what is he!" Scarlet laughed and I couldn't help it. I laughed, too. I liked Scarlet. "I'll get ye a few samples of the wine to try so ye will know what ye like. I'll be right back." She stood and straightened her outfit.

"Scarlet, please don't tell him I'm here. I'd like to surprise him."

"Yes, ma'am." She grinned and took off for the bar.

I pursed my lips for a moment and leaned back in my chair. I crossed my arms over my chest and watched Clive behind the bar. He tossed the alcohol and poured drinks. He was in his element. His black shirt was short sleeved... and his arms? Good lord, his arms were big. I wondered if he lumbers wood.

Look who's stereotyping now.

Shut up.

Scarlet came back to my table and slid her tray with five small vials of wine.

"Okay, Miss. May I ask yer name?"

"As long as you don't tell Clive what it is."

Her brows rose and she smirked. "He didn't get yer name?" I shook my head and grinned.

"Well, it is safe with me."

"Abby. Abby Masters."

"Well, Abby Masters, allow me to officially welcome ye to Scotland." She winked and took a seat next to me. "Here are five samples of Syrah, Malbec, Zinfandel, Merlot, and Cabernet Sauvignon. How familiar are you with each?"

"I'm good, I think. I'll try the Merlot first."

Scarlet nodded and handed it over. "Clive actually brought this one back from California. He has a distributor there now."

"Is that so?" I asked and took the Merlot. I sipped it and swallowed. "Nice."

She nodded. "Here is the Syrah. This one is best paired with steak or pretty much any wild game."

The wine in the glass was beautiful. It was so dark and when I smelled it, I smiled. I brought the small glass to my lips and tasted the spicy flavor of the Syrah. Spicy did not begin to explain the sensation that exploded on my pallet. I was in love. "Oh Scarlet, definitely my favorite!"

"Excellent!" Scarlet continued walking me through the different wines Clive had experimented with. The man had a natural talent, that was certain.

After I sampled all five of the wines, I asked for a bottle of the Syrah. Scarlet also took an order for some finger foods. She was a smart girl. All this alcohol and no one to share it with? I definitely needed food. I would be here for a while. Good thing I had Nick's card in my purse. He'd definitely receive a call from me later for a ride back to my hotel.

Scarlet came to my table with the wine and a single glass. She twisted in the corkscrew and pulled. The lid popped and she handed me the cork. "Abby, there is something ye need to be aware of. It is customary for Clive to visit any table that orders a bottle of his best. The Syrah is his best, by far. I'm warning ye so yer not surprised. He'll be by shortly." I suddenly felt panicked. I'm not sure why, but I did. My eyes widened and I started to shake my head. Scarlet waved her hands at my obvious surprised expression, "I promise, I did not announce it was ye who bought the wine."

"He doesn't know my name, remember?"

"Oh yes!" Scarlet grinned and poured my first glass. She glanced behind her then back to me. "He'll be over soon. Ye look beautiful, by the way." She winked.

I grinned. "Scarlet, I would love to hang out with you sometime when you're not working."

"Oh, I would love that! Okay Abby, I need to tend to my other tables, but I'll be back by soon! Good luck!"

Great. Clive would be coming by. I felt my heart quickly pick up in my chest. Maybe I'm kidding myself to think he would remember me. Maybe my own feelings were a crush.

Maybe.

I didn't want to wait to find out. Scarlet was talking to him behind the bar and he nodded at her with a smile. Before he could look my way, I quickly got up from my table and scrambled away. I needed somewhere to go.

Bathroom.

I looked to my left then my right and felt myself beginning to panic.

What the hell is wrong with you, Abby? This is not you!

Clive turned my direction and I quickly turned around, putting my back to him. I'm sure there were many other blondes in Scotland. I would be just another one of them, right?

I glanced to my right and saw a bright light of colors. It was the jukebox. Next to it, the bathroom. My saving grace.

I took in a deep breath, grabbed my purse, and then made a beeline for the bathroom.

"Excuse me, Miss?" I heard Clive's voice behind me. I didn't care; I kept walking. I did not want to see him, at least not yet. This is only my first day... no, I slept the first day away. This was my second day here. I needed to experience things before I got wrapped up... or wrapped around... a hot man!

The bathroom door closed behind me and I exhaled the breath I had been holding. A woman washing her hands eyed me for a moment. She raised a single brow then dried her hands. She was tall and thick, like a female version of a lumberjack.

"Someone messing with the likes of ye?" she asked me.

"What? Oh no, it is nothing like that, but thank you."

"For what?" She walked closer and looked me over. I suddenly felt self-conscious.

41

"For asking, I guess. Excuse me." I side stepped around her and made my way to the sink.

She shrugged and walked out. I ran the water in the sink and washed my hands. I sighed and looked at myself in the mirror. "What am I doing?" I shook my head and lowered my gaze.

Who am I trying to convince here? I thought I didn't need my family or my friends back home. I would give anything to have Lexi or Makayla here with me... gossiping about the sexy Scottish God waiting for me outside. My heart hurt at the longing of my friends.

Doesn't matter. You fucked that up by fucking Blaine.

Shut up!

I sighed and squared my shoulders. "What the fuck ever. New Abby, new me." I pulled my lip gloss from my purse and applied the cherry flavor to my lips, then put it away. I smiled and raised a single brow.

"I'm Abby fucking Masters." I tossed my hair and inhaled deeply. "I can do this."

I walked toward the bathroom exit then exhaled slowly. I pushed the door open and found my table empty, save for my full bottle of wine. I stepped out to a waiting Scarlet. She glanced to me and grinned.

"Run away much?" she asked.

"Not often. Where did he go?" I looked around the bar but could not see Clive for the super tall men in my way. "Scarlet, what do you feed your men here? Shit, they're all so damn tall!"

She laughed and shook her head. "I wish I knew. Who are ye to talk? You're fucking gorgeous and tall! Look at ya!"

Right about that time is when a few of the males in earshot turned around. Someone whistled a cat call.

"Ignore them," Scarlet insisted. "They're harmless. I'm here every day, never had an incident. Clive would never allow it."

"He's protective of you?" I asked, feeling a little more relaxed being stared it.

"Yes, but not so much me. He's protective of his business. Anyone dare start any shenanigans and he would kick them out. Eighty-six them from the bar."

I nodded. The music had quieted down and I felt fidgety. "So... jukebox plays?"

"Yup." She winked. "See ye at yer table." She left my side. I suddenly felt completely exposed. This is so not me. I'm the confident one. I'm the one always in control. Well, I was... but I'm out of my element here.

I bit my lip and one of the gigantic men in front of me grinned. Well, here goes nothing. I pulled some change from my purse and made my way over to the jukebox. There was nowhere to slip money into it.

"How the hell do you pay for tunes?" I looked all around it then sighed.

"Just push the button and it plays," came a voice next to me. I looked over at the tall man who was just grinning my way.

"Thank you." I pulled my hair behind my ear and turned back to the music.

"I'm Ed." He leaned onto the jukebox and held out his hand. I glanced at it then smiled at him.

"Nice to meet you, Ed." I shook his hand then released it.

"So, American?"

I raised a single brow. "What gave it away?"

He chuckled. "Visiting family or holiday?"

"Holiday." I pressed B36 on the machine. The White Stripes' drumbeat to "Seven Nation Army" began to play.

"Rock lover?"

I sighed. "Not so much anymore." Thoughts of Blaine crossed my mind and I quickly dismissed them... like he'd dismissed me. The asshole.

I pressed C54, then D45.

"Would ye like to dance?"

I glanced at Ed and blinked. "To 'Seven Nation Army'?" He

nodded. "Maybe next song. Thank you, though." I smiled and turned away from him. Ed grabbed my arm gently and pulled me back.

"Ahh now, c'mon, let's dance." He grinned and pulled me back.

"I believe I told you no. Let me go. Now." I didn't like this Ed guy and I definitely did not like being pulled around. I may be on foreign soil but I'll be damned if I am going to be treated like a second-class citizen.

"Fuck sakes, Ed. Let the woman go." Scarlet's voice broke the tension. I pulled my arm away, then gave a sharp smile and turned away from him. I rolled my eyes.

I walked back to my table and for the moment, forgot about everything else. That is until I saw my bottle of wine. Scarlet was next to me in a flash. She slipped her arm through mine.

"Ed is harmless. He's a good guy, just a little aggressive."

"A little?" I huffed and took a seat. "I would love to dance, just not with him." Panic! At The Disco came over the speakers, my next song selection of "Miss Jackson". I grinned.

"Can you dance now? I love this song!" I bounced a little in my step and Scarlet laughed.

"I get two breaks each shift. I haven't taken either so he owes me." She unwrapped her apron and set it on the table, then offered her hand for mine. "Shall we?"

"Oh, we so shall!" I laughed and Scarlet pulled me toward the dance floor.

The music was loud; it drowned out my thoughts and allowed me to be... me. I needed this. I needed to let go, regardless of Ed, Clive, or anyone else. I put my arms in the air and moved my body to the sound of Brendon Urie singing about a woman who stole the souls of men. It sounded familiar.

About half way through the song, I felt someone's hands on my arms from behind. Dancing in clubs in Dallas and Fort Worth, this was common. Here in Scotland, well I'm not so sure about club etiquette.

His hands moved down my arms to my waist and I felt his body's presence right behind me. I glanced at Scarlet and her eyes widened, then she grinned. Whoever this mystery man was behind me, he was breathing slightly on my neck. Damn, it was nice.

I closed my eyes and leaned into him. One song and it was almost over. I could stop dancing and just walk away. No harm, no foul. Right? Right.

Then the music changed. It didn't stop. It kept going... and so did we. INXS' "Need You Tonight" played over the speakers. I loved this song.

I dipped my body slightly and continued to dance with whoever was behind me. He leaned in and sang, "I need ye tonight, 'cause I'm not sleeping, there's something about ye girl, that makes me sweat."

I grinned and tried not to laugh. Having a Scottish man singing INXS lyrics in my ear was... well, it was hot! I turned around and shock didn't begin to cover what I felt. I took a few steps back and felt my heart race slightly.

"Clive?"

"Darling, why did ye stop dancing? Shit, that was hot! C'mon!" He chuckled and continued to dance.

I felt myself blush and I shook my head. "You are incorrigible!" I turned away from him and left the dance floor.

"Oh c'mon, darling! Come back!" He chuckled again. I looked over my shoulder and he made a pleading, begging motion. "I AM NOT ASHAMED TO DROP TO MA KNEES!"

At this, the other men in the bar began to cheer him on. Scarlet was at my side in a second.

"What in the hell?" I asked. "Why didn't you tell me?"

She grinned. "He told me not to. I like ye, Abby, I do, but he's ma boss and well... we've just met. I'm sorry, he wins this one." She grinned again. "Ahh, go over there. Look! He's begging for ye, Abby. He's fucking begging!"

45

"No." I wanted to smile. I wanted to laugh. No one had ever done this for me, but dammit, he embarrassed me with the begging.

"Don't be like that. He's a good guy. Go on. He's picking up the tab for ye wine."

"What?" I asked. "I thought he didn't know it was me?"

"He didn't, until he saw ye with Ed here. He asked me if ye were the Syrah purchase, and I said yes. He immediately came out and then... well, he danced with ye. Shit, Clive has moves!" She danced in place and raised her arms above her head.

I grabbed Scarlet's arms to get her attention. "Hell yeah, he does," I mumbled. She grinned at me, "Oh shit, did I say that out loud?" She nodded and giggled.

"Go dance, woman!" she demanded.

I sighed and pretended to roll my eyes. "Fine."

Clive was now on his knees, his hands pressed together and his eyes were closed. "Please, sexy woman, come back to me! Show me how ye want ye cream whipped!"

I couldn't hold it in any longer. I laughed out loud then shook my head. "You are totally unbelievable."

Clive stood up and closed the distance. "C'mere, ye." He pulled me close and hugged me. "I'm glad ye found me."

Poison's "Ain't Nothing But A Good Time" played next. This was not one of my song selections but damn if it didn't excite me. I smiled. "Me, too, although to be honest," I pulled back to look him in the eyes, his beautiful emerald green eyes, "I didn't realize you were Patterson Distillery."

"Does that change things?" He asked as he tilted his head. I shook mine no. "Good." He pulled me closer again, "don't need nothing, but a good time, how I can I resist?"

I giggled. I felt his hand move my hair to the side and he leaned in closer.

Someone yelled out, "GET'ER, CLIVE!"

I felt him chuckle next to me. "Please, darling, tell me yer name."

My hands moved down to his chest. My god, he was strong. I felt his sculpted chest under my palms and my mind began picturing him naked. I met his gaze and it was a little intense. My god, this man was... hot. How did I not see this on the plane, right next to him? I smiled and felt a blush touch my cheeks. "Abby. Abby Masters."

"Well, Abby Masters, may I officially welcome ye to Scotland." With that, Clive leaned in and kissed me.

7

I pushed against Clive's chest and ended the kiss… his intense, warm, and luscious lips sent thrills through my body and between my thighs. My god, he smelled so good. I wanted to kiss him again, but this was not why I came here.

"Oh darling, I'm sorry," he started. "But if I offended ye, I didn't do it right," he chuckled. "Do I need to do it again?"

I shook my head and grinned. "No, first time was… it was… no, Clive," I stepped back, "I'm good."

"Well, I'm not. I need another one." He waggled his brows and leaned in. He was met with my palm on his face. "What? Why?" He grinned.

"We just met!" I exclaimed with a grin.

"Well if I must, I have no issue making out with ye hand and taking it home later." He winked and pulled my hand closer. He made something like a kissy face toward it then glanced at me as he licked my palm.

"Oh my god, stop!" I laughed and tugged on my hand.

"No way. This hand is coming home to molest me tonight!" He chuckled then winked at me.

"Clive, seriously, let me go. I need to go wash my hands now."

"Oh right. So where was ye hand just before ma tongue?" He raised a single brow.

Oh, I could have fun with this.

"Well? I was in the bathroom and you ran out of hand soap. The food here hasn't agreed with me, so…" I turned side to side like an innocent child and smiled to him. His grin faltered to a frown and he blinked.

"Ye must be joking. Tell me yer joking… please, Abby!" Clive glanced at Scarlet, who had bit her lip to keep from laughing. "Scarlet! Is the bathroom out of soap?"

She shook her head no and finally let out the laugh that she had been holding in. "Boss, seriously! Ye are too easy!"

"I licked her bloody hand, woman!" Clive yelled. I laughed and took another step back.

"That'll teach you," I said.

"That'll teach me what?" he asked. "To not lick ye, ever, anywhere?" His grin returned and this time, it was mischievous. Oh, I saw where this was going.

No, I can't, not like this. I liked Clive. He was fun, so was Scarlet. We all may have just met but I didn't want to start out the adventure of finding myself by fucking a tall, gorgeous, fit Scottish man who looked damn sexy in a kilt. Good lord, what is it with the men over here?

"Clive," I lowered my voice as I spoke his name. "Please, don't." I turned and made my way back to my table. I sat down and crossed my legs. Glancing over at him, he was watching me, probably curious why I had walked away.

Was he used to getting whatever woman he wanted? Was he like Blaine or was he more down to earth and a one-woman man? I had no idea and the thought gave me a headache.

He made his way over toward my table, Scarlet rushing up behind him.

"I have her table, boss. I'll take care of her."

"Right, go check the loo. Make sure it's fit." His eyes never left mine as he stood at my table.

"I'm sure it's fine, Clive. I was just..."

"Go!" he ordered Scarlet. She nodded then glanced to me. I gave her a brief smile and she turned and left.

He slowly made his way across the floor. He had a look of sincerity that touched me in the wrong places. The way he breathed on my neck, when he kissed me, and even when he licked my hand...

"I didn't... I didn't know this was your place," I began, "I wanted to get out to see the area and I picked up the flyer. My cabbie spoke highly of your family."

"He did, did he?" He motioned to the chair across from me. "May I?" I nodded. "Well, regardless of how ye got here, I'm glad ye are here. Personally," he leaned in and lowered his voice, "I haven't been able to get ye out of ma head."

I smiled... and blushed. It had been a very long time since a man had made me blush, at least as often as Clive had. "I've been thinking about you as well."

He slid over into the chair next to me. He rested his elbows on the tabletop and interlaced his fingers. "Ye have?" He grinned. "Dirty thoughts?" He waggled his brows.

I laughed and shook my head. "No, not dirty. Just... thinking."

"Is it a mystery I need to guess?"

I shook my head no and crossed my arms over my chest. "Why were you in Texas, Clive?"

"Oh, I wasn't really in Texas, love. I was there on a connecting flight from California." He sat back in his chair and interlaced his fingers on his head. His arms were thick and the sleeves rose slightly on each side. He had a tattoo on his right bicep that I could see peeking out. "I have a vineyard out there, and I'm building a distribution center as well." He paused for a moment and cleared his throat. "Abby?"

"What?" I flinched slightly and realized I had been staring at his arms. My mouth was slightly ajar and I held my breath. Clive smiled again. "So, umm, you said distribution center in California?"

He nodded and brought his arms down. "Want to see it, love?"

"Umm, see what?" I bit my lip. I assumed he meant his ink, but when he said *see it*, I had no idea what he was referencing.

He chuckled and reached for the sleeve on his right arm, then pulled it up. He brought his thick arm around and slightly flexed it. "Had this done a few years ago when I took over the business. It's a Celtic design."

It went around his bicep. It most likely meant something to him.

"Does it have meaning behind it? The design, that is?"

He nodded. "All of ma tats have meaning. I don't get work done just for shits and grins."

"Okay, so what does it mean?"

"The loops through here," he pointed to the top, "mean strength. The points and edges along the top and bottom," he pointed and I tilted my head, listening, "mean family and loyalty. We're very close as a family and community."

I nodded. "I do not have any tattoos. I was going to go into modeling once upon a time, but due to unforeseen circumstances, that didn't work out." I wanted to reach over and touch his work, run my fingers across his skin. As I was about to work up the courage to do just that, he lowered his sleeve.

"So why didn't ye? The modeling, that is. What happened?"

I sighed. How do I tell this story without getting too personal? I glanced at the ground and a single brow rose.

"Abby," I glanced up to meet his gaze. "If it's too hard to tell, don't."

I smiled. "Thank you, but it's not that. I was wanted by a few companies."

"I can see why. Yer bloody fucking gorgeous." He winked and I smiled again.

51

"Thank you for that." I pulled my hair behind my ear and re-crossed my legs toward him, then leaned on the table. "I was about to sign with an agency in Manhattan, then things changed. Someone came in that... well, they sort of ruined it for me."

"Ahh, someone with a different look? What is the term, edgier?"

"Something like that." Movement caught my attention and I found Scarlet waving across the floor. She smiled and mouthed, *you okay?* I nodded and she gave me a thumbs up. Clive followed my gaze and furrowed his brows at her. She flipped him off and I laughed.

"That woman!" He chuckled and turned back to me. "So, what else do ye do, Abby Masters from Texas?"

I shrugged. "These days, not too much. Unlike yourself, my family is not that close." I lowered my gaze, "I'm an only child. My father is a self-made, successful businessman and my mother... well... let's just say she's not happy with life right now."

Slowly, I glanced up to him and was surprised to find him watching me. His expression was curious, but not disappointed. I've come to find that those that love their family are ones I usually have a hard time interacting with. They don't get it. Then again, I don't get what they have, either.

"So ye father, he made his money and wasn't born into it? Some folks tend to say those who were born into it become pompous. Others appreciate the hard earned money." Clive leaned forward and continued the conversation. I was relieved he didn't ask about my mother. Typically, that's what I get first.

Where's your father in all this?

Why is your mother a drunk?

Oh well, that explains a lot about you. The first time I heard this I slapped that bitch. Fuck you for judging me.

"Yes, he holds a high powered position. He's the President."

"I see. And do ye enjoy business, Abby?" He reached for a napkin and fumbled with it for a bit.

"Honestly, not in the least." I shrugged. "I don't get involved. I just stand when told, pose when told, and smile when told. I help out in my father's office when he needs it, but otherwise, I'm nowhere around it."

"And yer mother, she's good with ye, aye?" He watched me for a moment then shoved the napkin away. Clive leaned forward and rested his elbows on his thighs. "If I'm asking too many questions, feel free to tell me to bugger off."

I grinned slightly and tilted my head. How did I answer this? Honestly? Not tell the entire truth? "Well? If I were to be honest with you about my family, it might scare you off. I'm not sure I'm quite ready to go there with a stranger."

He chuckled. "Abby, I licked yer palm. We're not that strange to each other." I raised my brows and grinned. I was about to argue the point and he held up his hand. "No, don't, I know. We're strange. Here," he held out his hand, palm up. "Lick mine. We'll call it even."

"What?" I looked at his hand then back at him. "I'm not going to lick your palm, Clive."

"Ahh c'mon, it's clean." He winked then reached for my hand. He ran his thumb over the top of it and didn't break eye contact with me. "Stay and help me close up the night, aye?"

"If you want me to, sure. What do you need me to do?"

"Nothing darling, yer doing it. Sit here and allow me to watch ye." He leaned in closer and I could smell his aftershave. He was divine. I wanted to run my hands through is thick hair and grab it. I wanted to pull his head toward me and kiss him. I wanted his lips on my body.

What the hell, Abby?

"You like to watch people?" I couldn't believe I just asked that. Maybe in Scotland watching people would be sexual, like voyeurism. Holy hell.

"Only if they allow me to." He winked and quickly leaned in

and kissed my cheek. "I'd only watch if ye allow me to, which one day, I hope ye do."

Oh my god. OH MY GOD. Slowly, I turned my face toward him and he hadn't moved. He tilted his head slightly and our eyes met. My lips parted and more than anything, I wanted his lips on mine. I didn't care if we'd just met. This man, this god-like man, made me wet and I was trying not to squirm in my seat.

"What's the matter, Abby? Did I nail it?"

"Not yet." Holy shit, did I say that out loud?

He chuckled. "Maybe one day soon, I can."

A moment passed between us and nothing was spoken. No one moved. As I was about to break the intense staring, he cupped my cheeks and kissed me again. He held it for a moment then as he pulled away, I grabbed his shirt and pulled him back.

I decided enough was enough. I took control and my tongue glided across his lips. He groaned and opened his mouth for me. Clive deepened the kiss and became quite aggressive. Even though I thought I was in control, I soon realized it was he. This kiss had my heart beating faster, my panties wetter and the throbbing between my legs quickened. I wanted more than anything to climb onto his lap, right now.

Until I heard someone cheer, "GET HER!" At this, Clive ended the kiss as he smiled against my lips, then pulled away.

"This is far from over, Abby." He grinned and kissed me once more before he pulled away. He stood up and his crotch was right in front of me. The man was sporting a full hard on and it was showcased. His kilt was definitely showing his package.

I covered my lips and tried not to laugh. I looked up to him and found him smirking.

"Aye, you did it, love. You gave me a fucking throbber." He winked then left my table. Some clapped his back and the man named Ed watched me for a moment, the look of disappointment evident.

"Oh ma god, Abby!" Scarlet's voice came out as a squeal. "What happened? He has... oh Abby! He's hard!" She laughed and sat down in the seat he had just vacated.

"Well, I can see he wears it traditionally." I glanced at Scarlet and shook my head. "Oh Scarlet, I'm in so much trouble." I grinned and looked at where Clive was standing. He winked at me from behind the bar and poured a man a beer.

8

*M*idnight came and the crowd was still busy in Hitter's Bar. Clive was still making drinks and I stayed at my table sipping on my delicious wine. Scarlet had given me some finger food a few hours ago, food I've long since devoured. A few times, when it would quiet down, Clive came over to check on me. He would go as far as leaving a kiss on my cheek.

India.

I would be leaving soon. Then I would be on my way to Australia. I couldn't ask Clive to wait for me. Hell, we just met. He was a sexy, strong, well-established man here in Scotland. Any woman would be proud to call him hers. He wanted to spend the evening with me and for the first time in as long as I could remember, I was scared to have sex.

I didn't want to ruin a potential friendship between us. I didn't want to be hurt, or hurt him. Would it hurt him? Probably not, he's a guy.

"Wow, I'm really over thinking this shit," I told myself.

Scarlet came to my table with a smile. "We should be closing up in about twenty minutes. Clive is beginning to push people out with last call."

I nodded. "Sounds good. Should I wait outside?"

"Not on yer life," Clive called behind me. "Ye don't get to leave unless it is with me. Fresh meat out there? Not happening."

Not sure what to say to that, I looked at Scarlet for answers. She simply shrugged with a grin. "I don't blame him," she began. "Men are drunk off their arses. No telling what they'll do." With that, she left my table and began to clean up the ones just vacated.

Hands gripped my shoulders, large, dominating hands. Lips were next to my ear and I could only smile. "I know what I want to do." Clive kissed my neck then released me.

I turned and watched him as he walked away.

Shit.

I knew I was in so much trouble.

~

*I*t was almost one in the morning. I was tired, but I was also very much awake. I had no idea what Clive had in mind for us, but my mind was all over the place in thoughts.

What if we make out?

What if he wants to have sex?

What if I say no?

Will I be able to say no?

Lord, help me.

Scarlet pulled me from my thoughts when she handed me a slip of paper. "Here's ma number. When ye are free, phone me. I would love to take ye shopping."

I smiled. "Thank you! I would love that." I placed the paper in my purse and sipped on the last of my wine. I felt pretty lit. I wanted to giggle, so I did.

"Will ye be okay to get home?" Scarlet tilted her head in concern.

"I think so. Clive asked me to wait with him. Maybe he'll take me home." I grinned sheepishly. "Maybe we'll make out!" I gasped then covered my lips. "I didn't mean to say that."

She shook her head and waved off my statement. "Maybe he'll take ye home with him." She winked.

This sobered me only slightly. As much as I would love to go home with Clive, I know this would not work out well in my favor. "Does he do that often?"

Scarlet's brows rose in surprise.

"Well? Does he? I don't know him well enough to know, you know?" I shrugged.

She shook her head. "Not really ma place to kiss and tell, now is it?" She turned away from me with a grin and headed toward the door.

"Bitch!" I yelled.

Scarlet turned back and blew a kiss to me. I pretended to catch it and place it in my make believe pocket. She laughed and headed out the door.

"Be safe getting home," Clive told her, then closed the door behind her. He locked it then stood there for a moment. He glanced over at me then leaned against the door. "Ye ready to head out?"

I shrugged. "I suppose so." I stood and weaved slightly on my feet. "Whoa." I held my hands out as if to steady myself.

He chuckled. "I got ye, darling." Clive came to my side, wrapped an arm around my waist, and pulled me close.

"You smell good." I grinned and leaned into him.

"Well, thank ye. Shall we, ma dear?" He motioned for the door.

My mind wasn't thinking when I nodded. "Where are we going? Your place or mine?"

He chuckled. "Ma car is here. I'll take ye to ma home and give ye ma bed. Ye appear pretty inebriated."

"No, I'm not!" I protested. I could think for myself, sort of. I just had a hard time standing. "Hey, what does Scotland feed their men? Because all of y'all are so big and strong!"

"Is that right?" He chuckled and helped me out the back door. A shiny black Audi was under the parking lamp in the lot. The headlights blinked twice and he opened the passenger door. "Get yer fine ass inside. I'll take good care of ye."

"I hope you do. I'm fragile, you know." Where the hell that came from, I had no idea. First, we kiss, then I get drunk, and now he's taking me home with him. Great. So much for following through with my plans for finding myself.

He closed my door and walked around the front of the car. The interior smelled like him. It was nice. I could sleep out here... I think.

Clive opened his door and the dome light came on. He climbed in and looked over at me before closing the door. He whistled. "Damn baby, ye have nice legs." He shook his head.

"Thank you." I felt myself blush slightly... or maybe it was the alcohol. I'm not quite sure.

He closed his door and started up the car. He pulled out on the road and took off. I had no idea where I was or where we were going. I absently thumbed through my purse and felt Nick's card inside it. If I got in a pinch, I had someone I could call.

I hope.

"So," Clive began, "here we are, again, side by side in some sort of transportation. Plane, train, car... maybe next time it'll be to Texas."

"Oh, do you plan on going to Texas?" I looked at him and found him smiling. "What? Why are you smiling like that?"

"Had it occurred to ye I might want to visit ye in Texas?"

I hadn't thought of that. I nodded and turned to look out my window. "Clive, you should know something."

"Don't, it's okay." He reached over and squeezed my hand. I looked at it, then at him.

"You don't know what I was going to say."

"I don't need to know," he started. "Ye are here with me now, and that's all I want. Just yer time while I can have it."

"But Clive..."

"No, Abby, no. Let's just have fun while ye are here. I don't want to know when ye have to leave. Can we just have a good time?" He pulled up to an intersection and stopped the car. No one was coming or going. Clive put his car in park. He turned to face me and his expression was serious.

"What are you doing?" I asked. I looked around the neighborhood and it seemed nice. It was residential and the homes looked beautiful, from what I could see in the middle of the night, that is.

Clive continued to look at me until he finally shook his head. "Nothing, we're doing nothing. Nothing that ye don't want to do while ye are here and nothing we can't do together. I'm not that kind of man, Abby. I like ye, and if truth be told, ye seem to like me as well." I smiled and knew this time that I was blushing. I was glad the darkness of the car disguised it. "Let's just have a good time while we can. Aye?"

I sighed and nodded. "All right." I continued to smile when he put the car into gear. The light had already turned green. He drove through the intersection and a short distance later, we pulled up to a large lit entrance gate.

The gate entrance was metal and had a P designed in the middle. I immediately assumed P was for Patterson. Who exactly was I in the car with? The gate was white with black painted tops. It had a modern edge feel.

Clive pushed the button to the window and after it rolled down, he reached through and punched in a series of numbers. A beep sounded and the gates began to open. He pulled through the entrance and when I glanced in my passenger side mirror, I saw the gate had begun to close behind us.

"May I ask where we are... exactly?" I turned to look at him.

An amused look covered his face... at least it appeared to be amusement.

"Abby, we are at ma home." He parked the car and glanced over to me. "You'll be staying the night with me tonight, love."

"No, Clive!" I had begun shaking my head when he stopped me.

"No love, it's not like that. I told ye, I'm not that guy. I have many guest rooms. Ye are welcome to any of them... although I prefer the one next to mine." He winked at me.

I stared at him for a long moment. I don't think I blinked. He cleared his throat and I finally looked away. I took in a breath when I realized I had been holding it.

This should be easy for me. I'm the one who would seduce any man I wanted... even ones who were off limits. I think a part of me enjoyed the game... the hunt. The moment I could see their weakness, I would pounce.

Now? I was in uncharted territories. I had no idea what to do, what to say, or even what was expected of me.

"Abby?" Clive asked. He reached over and took my hand, then gave it a gentle squeeze. "I promise, nothing will happen tonight," he shrugged, "aside from maybe another amazing kiss. Maybe a good night one, aye?" He raised his brows to me.

I had no idea what to say. I looked at my lap then toward his... holy shit. His mansion? Who the hell IS Clive Patterson?

"Right. Well, I'll go inside," I managed to say, "and we'll sleep," I glanced to him, "in separate rooms." He nodded a few times and waited for me to finish. I cleared my throat and looked back at his home. "Then tomorrow, you'll tell me who you are exactly, because this?" I motioned to his home, "is definitely not what I was expecting."

"And what did ye expect exactly, Abby? A bartender's home on a bartender's wages?"

"Okay wow, yeah, that sounded judgmental." I pulled my hand from his. "That is so not what I meant."

"Ahh, but it is what ye implied, aye?"

No one ever called me on my shit; especially a man I had just met... regardless if I was going home with him or not.

"Whatever. I'll stay the night then in the morning, you'll take me home. No, better yet, I'll call a cab to come pick me up. I have a name in my purse of someone to call."

"Whatever ye would like to do, love, but I assure ye, I have no plans to touch ye tonight, even if ye BEG me to."

I gasped and glared at him. He wore a smirk and more than anything, I wanted to slap him... and kiss him. Not necessarily in that order, either. "I assure you, sir, no kissing will be begged for unless it is from you!" I reached for my door and fumbled with the handle. I pulled it three times and it wouldn't open. "What the hell is with your blasted door? Let me out!"

He chuckled and reached for a button that unlocked our doors. "Ma lady, yer bedroom awaits."

I shook my head and quickly left the car, making sure to close the door hard behind me. I stared at the front entrance and steps stood in front of me. There were only maybe five of them, but right now, it seemed like there were fifty.

"Shall we?" Clive asked and stood next to me. The porch light came on and the entrance... oh, the entrance was beautiful. White exterior with black trimmings, like the front gates. It was stunning. The front door opened to a man looking out at us with a smile.

As a child, I watched movies where butlers would answer the door wearing a tuxedo. I'm not sure what to expect with Clive's servants. Considering the time, I wasn't surprised to see him in lounge like clothes. The man was older, maybe in his fifties. He had gray hair and he was balding. And he wore a smile that would light up any room.

"Mr. Patterson, you've brought us a guest!" The door opened wider. As I looked in past the man, all I could see was a foyer with brilliant white tile. I had half a mind to run through the mud just to track something in on the perfection.

"Yes, Douglas, we have a guest. Abby, this is ma butler, Douglas. He's been with ma family for quite a while. Douglas, this is the Lady Abby."

"Oh, no, just Abby," I insisted. I smiled at Douglas and held out my hand.

Douglas looked at my hand, then at me. He smiled and shook my hand. "The pleasure is mine, I assure ye." I noticed his accent was not as Scottish as Clive's and wondered where he was from. Then again, being with Clive's family a while, who knew?

"Douglas, could we set her up in the room next to mine?" Clive asked. I glanced between the two men and I quickly shook my head.

"Umm, Douglas, before you answer that, is there a room on the other side of the house? I'm afraid that..." I trailed off and watched Clive's grin slowly shift to a frown. "I'm afraid I snore. Like loud. Really loud. I might keep sleeping beauty awake."

Douglas chuckled. "Well, I assure you, Lady Abby, that the Master here does sleep quite heavily. He would not hear ye; however, if ye prefer to sleep elsewhere, I'll be happy to lead the way." Douglas waited for what I believed was approval from Clive... in the form of a single nod.

"Right, well I'll see ye in the morning then, Abby." He stepped forward and Douglas took a slight step back then turned around. Oh hell, he's giving us privacy. "Sleep well. If it is true that ye snore as loudly as ye are leading me to believe, I'm sure there's a way to prevent that," he lightly cupped my cheeks and tilted my face up, "by kissing ye." He pressed a soft kiss to my lips, "All night." Clive winked then leaned in and kissed me again. He lingered there for a moment then pulled away.

I wanted to grab for him. I wanted to pull him back. I wanted to take back my sleeping on the other side of this huge home. As I was about to speak up, Clive turned and shoved his hands in his pockets, then walked toward what I assumed to be his bedroom.

"Right, Lady Abby, when yer ready," Douglas offered.

I lowered my gaze and turned toward the butler with a soft smile. I nodded. "I'm ready. And please, just Abby."

After a long walk, which was probably just a few minutes but felt like thirty, we reached the room where I would be sleeping. Douglas opened the double doors and stepped inside.

"Lady... umm... Miss Abby, here is the room on the opposite side of the home. I hope ye find this pleasing?" He stood at attention with his hands behind his back.

I stepped inside and looked around. I knew I had died and landed in girly girl heaven! The king size bed had a canopy wrapped with sheer drapes. The pillows... my god, there were so many pillows! They were laid across the bed and I could probably make a bed just out of these. The room itself was easily the size of my entire hotel suite, and then some.

"Yer bathroom is just over here. This room has its own private quarters. I took the liberty of picking this one for yer use while yer staying with us. May I ask how long yer time will be, Madam?"

"Oh Douglas, honestly, I'm not sure." I had no idea how much to tell Douglas so I left my answer at that.

He nodded. "If ye need anything, pull this lever." He motioned to the velvet rope hanging by the bed.

"People really have and use these things?"

Douglas looked to me like I was a heathen for the breadth of a second... then it was gone and he smiled. "Yes, madam, we do use these. The home is quite large."

"Yes, I noticed that." I smiled and lowered my gaze. "Thank you, Douglas. I appreciate the service."

"Yes, madam." Douglas lowered his head slightly then raised it again. "Will there be anything else?" I shook my head and turned toward the bed. "Right, then. Sleep well and someone will fetch ye in the morning."

"Fetch me?" I asked.

"Yes, gather ye for breakfast."

"Oh, I don't know if…"

He interrupted me with a smile. "Please, madam, trust me. You'll want to be here for breakfast. The Master may take up his… culinary skills in the kitchen."

Was he teasing me? He had grinned as if willing me to let me in on the joke he'd just told. I simply nodded and pretended to get it.

"Till the morning, Miss Abby. I hope ye enjoy the bed." Douglas closed the doors as he left my room.

It was so quiet. I wanted to sleep. It was a long day and after the alcohol consumption, I definitely needed to sleep off whatever headache I might have in the morning.

Not having my nightclothes handy, I took a chance and peeked through the dresser drawers in the room. Nightclothes, t-shirts, and shorts were provided for use. I smiled and made a mental note to thank whoever stocked the room with necessities.

I changed clothes and ventured into the bathroom. The light turned on as I entered the room and I gasped. The bathroom was huge! The sink space itself held three pedestal sinks.

"Why would someone need three sinks?"

I turned to the shower space and gasped again. A large Jacuzzi tub sat with a chandelier hanging over it. A mini fridge was next to the tub. Curious, I opened it and found it empty. Over in the corner was the shower. It was big enough for two people and it was enclosed with a glass sliding door. I had a momentary fantasy of Clive naked in the shower with me, holding my naked body against the glass.

I grinned… then I sighed. I quickly washed my face with the soap on the counter. I dumped all the pillows onto the floor and thought for a moment I might jump on them like a child would jump in a pile of leaves.

Instead, I pulled the covers down and slid between the satin sheets. They were cool next to my body and I found myself smiling. It didn't take long for sleep to take me under. Images of Clive and his smile... and our kiss... tormented my mind as I fell into unconsciousness.

9

H is hand moved up my body from behind as lips sucked on *my ear lobe. My breath came out in a rushed rhythm as it fogged the glass in front of me. His hands grasped my breasts and he squeezed. His chest pressed against my back. My body was squeezed between him and the shower wall. He lifted my leg and rested it on the side of the stall, then his fingers began to move between my folds. He pressed against my clit and rubbed it. I moaned and tilted my ass toward him.*

His other hand moved to my neck and he pulled me back, pulling me against his body. "I'm going to fuck ye, love. I'm going to fuck ye now."

He reached between us and pressed the head of his cock against my entrance. He pushed and hell if he didn't fill me.

"Clive..." His name was on my lips and I gasped. He pulled back and begun to thrust. He palmed my ass and squeezed. Fuck, he's going to make me cum.

I gasped again and suddenly sat up in bed. I glanced around the room and thought for certain I had been having sex with Clive and not... dreaming it. I fell back on the bed with a groan.

~

*a*fter I showered and dressed myself in last night's clothes, I pulled my hair back and stared in the mirror. I did not have my essentials with me. I never, ever let anyone see me without my make-up.

"Well, you're shit outta luck, Abby." I rolled my eyes at myself and thought back to the dream I'd had of Clive. The way he dominated my body, the way he took control... hell, it was always me in control. I couldn't let my guard down to anyone and let them have control.

It's how I kept anyone from hurting me. I held them at arm's length. I controlled what happened to me, therefore, no one could have the opportunity to hurt me... or break my heart.

I shook my head and walked out of the room. Not knowing if Douglas was waiting for me, I mean, why should he be? I reached for the velvet rope and gave it a tug. No sound emitted and I wondered if it worked. I gave it a moment and thought about tugging it again when I heard a knock at the door.

Slowly, I opened it and peeked out. "Douglas?"

"Miss Abby?" He asked with a smile. "I trust ye slept well?"

I had sex with Clive in my sleep. It was amazing. "Yes, thank you, I did. I, umm... don't have my make-up or anything with me."

"Ahh, there's no need to hide yer beauty behind make-up, ma lady."

"So you say," I teased. I opened the door fully and watched as Douglas' brow rose.

"Did you find the clothes in the closet not to yer liking or size?"

"Honestly? I did not look. I do not plan to outstay my welcome, Douglas, but thank you."

"All right then, and you're welcome, ma lady. Now, if you'll please follow me?" Douglas turned and headed away from my room. I sighed and followed. Soon, the smell of breakfast, specifically bacon, filled the air. My stomach growled and Douglas glanced over with an amused look.

"What?" I whispered. He grinned and shook his head. We stepped into the kitchen and Clive... well, he was shirtless, and in a pair of baggy sweats that barely clung to his very fit, very strong body. I felt myself biting my lip. My dream of him had nothing on what I was seeing now. He had a tattoo of a cross over the right side of his shoulder with a symbol in the middle of it. It was huge and beautiful... like Clive.

"May I present Lady Abby?" Douglas caught me off guard with the introduction. When Clive turned to face us, his bare chest exposed, I felt my face heat up. I wanted to turn around, but I found my feet glued to the floor. I heard Douglas chuckle as he turned to leave. "Breathe, ma lady," he whispered. I managed to glance his way... and maybe glare slightly.

Clive grinned. "Good morning, love. I'm cooking breakfast... well, I'm trying to cook, that is." He chuckled and his left hand grabbed the back of his neck, stretching his chest. I had to be careful not to drool.

I swallowed and finally inhaled. "I see that." I lowered my gaze to keep myself from staring at him. I slowly closed my eyes and shook my head. "I'm sorry I'm not more... presentable. I feel like a peasant girl, thrown into her majesty's court."

His bare feet came into my view as Clive stood in front of me. "Look at me," he said. "Abby, look at me." I shook my head.

"I have no clean clothes, no make-up and I'm so not ready to be seen." Some of my mother was in my words, some of it was me.

Clive touched my chin and lifted my head. "Look at me." My eyes were closed and reluctantly, I finally looked into his. His beautiful green eyes stared into mine. Patience, kindness, and something else I'm not that familiar with, understanding. "Ye are beautiful just as ye are. Don't change to be something someone else thinks ye should be. Just be ye."

I stared into his eyes and couldn't blink. I couldn't breathe. No one had ever said anything like that to me before. Clive was someone I could absolutely see myself spending a LOT of time with. And this was the thought that brought me back to reality.

You deserve everything you get, which is absolutely nothing.

My mother's words rang clearly in my head and it felt like a punch to my stomach.

"Clive," I whispered and reached for his hand. I pulled it away from my face and took a small step back. I blinked and looked around his shoulders. "Is something burning?"

"What? Oh hell!" He quickly turned around and rushed to the burners. He pulled away a skillet and set it aside. "See what ye do to me, woman?" He chuckled and grabbed a carafe of juice. "Fresh squeezed." He smiled and I nodded, then took a seat in the breakfast nook just to the side of the counter.

The kitchen was huge... just like everything else here. Every device, every pot and pan known to man seemed to be in this kitchen. Like the house, the kitchen was black and white. I wondered for a moment if this was his styling or if someone had done it for him.

Clive brought over the juice and set it down. He then gripped the chair next to me and tilted his head with a smile. "What can I slap ye plate with?"

I blinked. "Slap my plate?" I'm not sure if it was because he was almost naked or the term slap, but my mind went blank. Was he wearing underwear under those sweats? I bit my lip again.

"Do ye eat meat, Abby?"

"Oh, yes, I eat meat. I'm from Texas. We all eat meat." I grinned. He furrowed his brows in obvious confusion. "Seems I have a lot to teach you about southern women, Clive."

He chuckled. "Aye, seems ye do. I'll fix ye a plate, ye eat what ye like, aye?"

I nodded. As Clive walked toward the food, I couldn't help but stare at his ass... his perfectly round, squeezable ass. The dimples just below his waist, the area right above the ass cheeks, were in view. If Clive had on underwear, they would have shown here. My god, he was commando!

He turned to face me and stopped. He blinked and stood there. "Abby, is there something on me?"

"Umm, what?" I shook my head, getting myself out of my naked Clive daydream.

"The look on yer face. Ye need to know, I'm deathly afraid of spiders, love. Is there one on me?" The look of fear on his face was obvious. I tried hard not to smile, not to laugh, and not to flinch. He had a plate full of food he had prepared just for me. This was the sweetest thing anyone had ever done… and he was afraid of a spider. This man, this strong, sexy man, was scared of spiders.

I giggled and covered my lips. I shook my head a few times and tried not to laugh. Instead, I snorted. Loud.

"Seriously, Abby? Ye snort at ma fear? I shall remember this, love." Clive grinned and sighed with relief, then set the food in front of me, along with two serving plates.

"I'm so sorry, Clive," I giggled again, "Really, I am!"

"Right. And ye, love, have no fears of spiders?"

I shook my head. "Snakes, yes. Spiders, no. Snakes are the devil. They move with NO legs. Shit ain't right." I grabbed a piece of bacon and munched.

"Ain't right?" He questioned. I laughed. Hearing Clive try to speak in a southern accent while sporting a Scottish accent was one of the funniest things I've heard.

"Snakes are like the devil, Clive. 'Nuff said." I nodded.

"What is nuff, love? Is that like, enough?"

I grinned and nodded. "We have a long way to go to translate, it seems, when alcohol is not in the way."

"Oh love, alcohol did ye no favors last night. I barely under-stood a word ye said! Everything sounded like… gibberish."

I gasped then playfully slapped his arm. "I assure you, sir, the leader of my Cotillion classes would slap you with her white gloved hand!"

He grinned and nodded. "Touché, and understood."

~

 *W*e finished breakfast and Clive left me in the kitchen long enough to dress his gorgeous body. I made a mental note to become more acquainted with said body.

I thought the point of this trip was to find yourself, Abby. Not find yourself under someone?

Shut up!

I shook my head at the voice in my head. I sighed and stood in the foyer. The pictures on the walls looked like originals and not prints. At least they appeared like freshly dried oil paintings. Some were wooded park areas; others were of what could only be described as the heavens. I wondered for a moment what had gone through Clive's mind as he'd bought these pieces.

My mother used to enjoy attending art auctions. Until my father cut her off from the family funds. She'd bought a piece that he described as an expensive piece of shit. He thought a child had painted it. Paint had been splattered everywhere on the canvas.

"It spoke to me," she'd said.

"Well, you can speak to our attorney if you do that shit again," he'd retorted. I think that was the beginning of her downfall. I'm not certain, however.

"Ready, love?" Clive's voice brought me back to the present. He was now dressed in denim jeans that were almost fitted to his body. Damn. He wore a black fitted t-shirt that hugged his chest and arms.

My eyes drifted down his body and my brows rose. "I... Yes, I am." I smiled and my eyes met his. He smirked and chuckled.

"I can see that." He motioned toward the door. "Shall we?"

I lowered my gaze then hid my face behind a false cough, and nodded. We walked out toward a detached garage. I stood there for a moment and looked back toward the house, then at Clive.

"I thought I saw an attached garage last night?" I said.

He nodded. "You did. We're going this way today." He held out his elbow for me, like the gentleman he was apparently trying to be. I grinned and slipped my hand into the crook of his arm.

"Lead the way."

Half an hour later, we had arrived at my hotel. "Why does one man need so many cars, Clive? Honestly."

He chuckled. "Well, honestly," he told me in a mocking tone, "they're not all mine. Some are ma families; some are collection. This Mercedes and the Audi are mine. I fancy luxury cars." He winked at me.

"I can see that. You seem to fancy luxury in about everything that surrounds you."

Clive was quiet for a moment. I wondered if I had offended him. As I was about to speak up to apologize, he began. "Truth be told, love, it was not by choice. There's a story about me ye have yet to uncover."

I nodded and understood. I could appreciate that and I had been right; I had offended him. "Clive, I apologize. I did not mean to imply…"

He cut me off. "Nonsense. Don't worry yer beautiful self about that, ye hear me?" He looked toward me with a sincerity about him that made me want to hug him.

"All right. If we're telling back stories, there is quite the story about my life as well."

"Aye, will ye tell me about it?" He parked the Mercedes and turned it off. The car was very quiet and my heartbeat was all I could hear. I wasn't ready for this conversation, especially with someone I hardly knew.

Then again, hardly knowing someone could make him the perfect person. No judgments. No pretense of what to expect. No observations by others.

I sighed and shrugged. "Sure, why not?"

73

"Hmm," he watched me for a moment then shook his head. "No, not yet."

"Oh, okay. Why not?" I wasn't expecting this answer. Now I was curious.

"Ye are not ready." Clive opened his door and stepped out. I was really confused. How did he know whether I was ready or not? I followed suit and stepped out of the car.

"Excuse me? How would you know if I'm ready or not?" My hands pressed against my hips as I watched him cross over toward me. "You don't know anything about me."

"Exactly why ye are not ready. There is obviously something bothering ye, I can see it." He tapped the side of his head. "I'm a bartender and I'm also educated through university in areas other than liquor. I can see ye are hurting and, most likely, running from something. What that something is, well, time will tell, I suppose."

I am stunned. There are no other words to explain what I'm feeling. Maybe pissed. Maybe upset. "How dare you."

"How dare I? How dare ye," he countered. "Now, before we have our first fight and I demand we have make-up sex, let's get ye upstairs to clean up and get dressed. There are a few places I'd like to take ye today."

"No. You will leave. Do not pretend to know anything about me, Clive!" I turned and huffed toward the hotel. Who the hell did he think he was? He knew nothing about me but made pre-determined judgments. That is the most...

"Abby!"

Clive called after me and broke me from my thoughts. I shook my head and kept going. I felt my eyes water and dammit, this fucker would NOT make me cry.

Suddenly, I was pulled back against his body. His arms surrounded me and he held me close. His lips were by my ear and he whispered so softly, so reassuringly, "Abby, love, I apologize. Please, do not leave like this. I can see someone has hurt ye, cut ye deep. Allow me inside yer walls. I only wish to be here, nothing more."

"Clive, let me go!" I demanded. What the hell was he doing? I pulled against him but could not free myself. "Dammit, let me go, now!" I pulled again but his grip only tightened.

"No. Now ye listen to me. Yer trip to Scotland will be over soon. Ye may leave and be none the wiser for meeting me, or ye may gain some insight about yerself. Maybe some about me as well. Please, do not leave. Not like this."

I felt tears spring in my eyes. Now I was pissed. He was going to make me cry. I did not cry. I never cried, ever! No one made Abby Masters cry!

Well, except your mother.

And your father for not standing up for you.

And your friends for judging you.

Yeah, you're a piece of shit. Fuck him and get it over with.

"Clive, please, stop. Just... stop."

"Don't leave. Please stay," he whispered.

"I can't... I can't do this."

I'm not sure what happened, but Clive released me. However, I didn't move. I stood there, motionless. The wind blew against my body and my hair teased across my back. I sniffed and wiped my eyes. Slowly, I turned to face him. My eyes were still downcast. I couldn't look at him, at least not yet.

"I'm... I'm not a good person, Clive. I have done awful, despicable things to good people."

"Have ye killed anyone?"

This caught me off guard, which caused me to look up to him... into his eyes. He had a pleading look on his face and it hurt... it hurt badly. "Have I ever killed anyone? Well, no, I'm pretty sure I haven't. There have been times I wanted to, but no, no one has died at my hands."

He nodded. "Have ye ever slept with someone else's husband?"

Oh hell, I couldn't answer this one. Blaine wasn't technically married, but he was dating my, at the time, best friend. I sighed and lowered my gaze.

"Abby, did ye fuck someone's husband?" His tone had changed slightly.

I finally shook my head. "Husband? No. Best friend's guy? Yes." Slowly, my gaze moved up his body until I met his eyes. He did not look upset or ashamed. Clive actually shrugged.

"So what? They're not married. Have ye killed anyone's pet before?"

"What? You don't care I slept with my best friend's boyfriend?"

"Nope. I can't tell ye the times ma blokes' women have come onto me. I never fucked them, but it happens, Abby. Fuck them; it's yer past. Just don't let it become yer future. Now, did ye kill off any of ye pets or someone else's?"

I blinked. Who was this man? Was he so desperate for attention that he was willing to look past my obvious flaw of *what I can't have, I want*? I sighed and shook my head. "I love animals. I've never killed anything living, furry or otherwise."

"Not even a pet fish?" Clive grinned, which made me grin. I wanted to kiss him.

I shook my head and tried not to smile. "I only flushed them when they died."

"Right, then ye are good in ma book, Abby Masters." He winked. "Now, shall we get ye inside? Ye will spoil soon and honestly, a smelly woman is a turn off."

I feigned mock horror then laughed. "Let's go, but before we do, why did you hug me the way you did? No one..." I trailed off and shook my head. "Doesn't matter, let's go."

"No, it absolutely matters. I did it as a defensive mechanism. Do ye know of swaddling children?"

I nodded. "I do, but what does that have to do with this?"

"Sometimes we simply need the comfort of someone who cares for us surrounding us. I care about what happens to ye.

Something has happened and in time, when ye are ready, ye may tell me." He cupped my face and smiled at me.

Who was this man I had met on a plane in Dallas? Who was this man who ran a pub and distillery? Who was this man who saw right through my façade and made his way over my mental and emotional walls?

I wrapped my hands around his wrists and lowered his arms. "Let's go. I need to shower and you need to show me around town." Clive nodded and leaned in. He kissed me on the corner of my lips. My heart fluttered and my knees weakened.

~

*A*fter I showered, I wrapped my towel around my body. My clothes were on the counter and honestly, I did not want to dress. I wanted to walk into my bedroom and give myself to Clive. The only thing I feared right now was rejection.

He made a great point outside. I had a defense set up; I have had it for a long time. Protect myself. My rules. He'd managed to make it through my emotional barrier like it was simply made of air. Now, he sat in my room watching who knows what on the television. If I was to walk out there naked, I am confident he would fuck me now... but that would be it. A fuck.

I needed more, for the first time... ever; I needed more than that. This was no longer a chase for me. This was... hell, I don't know what it was.

I sighed and dropped my towel to the floor. I decided against venturing out in my birthday suit and opted to dress myself. I then quickly styled my hair.

My head began to hurt somewhat... and my heart hurt, too. Why? Clive had pushed on it somehow. Probably because no one had ever cared enough... not that I'd ever allowed them to. Partially my fault and I'd accept that.

I gripped the counter and braced myself. My chest began to

tighten, almost like it had outside my house. Panic? Anxiety? Both? Neither? Hell, I needed air and said air was right outside my bathroom door. He's wearing a black t-shirt that draped his body in a way that should be illegal. His pants hugged his ass... damn, that ass.

My head dropped forward and I sighed. "Hell, I have it bad." I pushed off the counter and stared at myself in the mirror. "What am I doing?" I shook my head and walked toward the door. I grabbed the handle and I felt like I was about to walk onto death row.

Dead man walking!

How did this man, this one single man, have this effect on me?

Because he sees right through you.

I sighed and turned the knob, and walked into the room.

Clive was lying across my bed. His ankles were crossed and he had the pillows bunched up behind him, one arm behind his head. He hadn't seen me yet, for which I'm thankful.

I took him in, like really took him in. He was tall, strong, thickly built. He had the reddest hair I've ever seen. His eyes, his green eyes, were so beautiful. His lips were full and luscious. His body was so sexy.

I felt my knees weaken again... and my panties get wet.

Fuck me, Clive. Fuck me.

Maybe he heard my thoughts, or maybe I sighed too loudly, but whatever it was, it caught his attention and he looked my way.

"Oh, hey, Abby." He sat up and tilted his head, then raised a single brow. "So, what is on yer mind? Do share because whatever it is, I think it is naughty." He waggled his brows.

I blushed, grinned, and lowered my gaze. "Am I that obvious?"

Clive stood and made his way over. I slowly looked up and he was directly in front of me. He touched my cheek and rested his other palm on the wall next to my head. He leaned in and his nose grazed my cheek. "Aye. Ye smell delicious." His hand slipped around my neck and he cupped the back of my head.

My breath caught in my throat and my heart rhythm picked up. His lips kissed my cheek. Then he kissed a little closer to my lips. I closed my eyes and my body was on fire. I should have walked out here naked.

I brought my hands up and rested one above his heart and the other on his forearm. Slowly, I slid my hand on his chest up to his neck. He kissed once more to the corner of my mouth. I exhaled an exasperated breath. I turned my head slightly toward his and his lips suddenly claimed mine.

They were hot and controlling. I've never allowed anyone to control me but my god, I would allow him to... at least at this moment.

He pressed his body against mine. He growled against my lips and the hand that was on the wall moved to my leg. He pulled it up and cupped my leg behind the knee. He pressed his erection against me and I gasped.

"Clive," I mumbled against his lips.

He reluctantly broke the kiss and rested his forehead against mine. Our breath was in rhythm and we were both trying to catch it. "Aye, love?"

"What would you have done if I walked out here naked?"

"Oh, ye are KILLING me, Abby. Killing me." He smiled and pulled away just enough to look into my eyes. "I would have taken advantage of said nakedness then made sure ye were okay with it, which obviously ye would be since ye would be naked."

I laughed and cupped his cheek with my hand. "Thank you for being honest." He winked. "We should go somewhere. I fear if we keep this up, I will be naked with you on my bed."

"And that would be so terrible?"

"Hardly, but I don't want to just fuck you, Clive. I want it to mean something. I want to know you."

He chuckled. "I can do that." He pulled away from me and adjusted himself in his pants.

I grinned then bit my lip.

"Fuck me," he raised a single brow. "That's sexy."

My brows rose. "What is sexy? What did I do?"

"That lip biting ye are doing. Fuck me, that's hot, love."

I grinned and bit my lip again.

Clive shook his head then bit his knuckle.

"Right, well, let's go," I stated. He grinned then ran his hand down his face.

10

*C*live took me around the township. We visited many sights, including a trip to Loch Ness. I told him I didn't believe there was a Loch Ness monster.

"A dark spot in the water does not make a monster, Clive."

"What, no Nessie, love?" He chuckled and squeezed me close to him. My body leaned against his and my arms were around his waist. Clive was warm. I enjoyed being close to him. It did not feel awkward or forced.

In past relationships, it had. Probably because whomever I was with, whomever I had chased to be mine, would finally relent... and I had them. After that, the game ended for me, as did the 'relationship'.

This was different, though, and I enjoyed the difference. Clive wanted me as much as I wanted him. He wasn't a game or a target. He was simply a man.

My god was he a man.

The wind picked up slightly and tousled my hair. He pulled it to the nape of my neck and held it there. I had the smallest of fantasies where Clive was tugging my hair while we made love. My heart sped up and warmth crested between my thighs.

He smiled at me and it was welcoming. Clive had taken the day off from his busy life at the bar and distillery to spend it with me. We both knew I would be leaving soon. He still refused to know what day that was.

"I'll know it has come the day ye don't come to ma bar," he paused for a moment and kissed my forehead, "ma home, or otherwise."

I nodded and kept the dates to myself. I didn't have the heart to tell him it would be in a few days.

~

*W*e made it back to his place and he parked in the detached garage. It was quiet. The music was turned off and neither of us were speaking. I felt nervous... I wasn't sure if he wanted me to stay or if this would be our last night together.

Do we sleep together?

Do we not and wonder down the road, what if?

Do I kiss him? Should I let him kiss me?

My fingers ringed in my lap; hearing Clive's chuckle brought me from my thoughts.

"What's the matter?" He asked me. His fingers lightly traced my cheek to my ear.

"Just... I don't know where to begin." I shrugged slightly. "I mean," I sighed and turned to face him. "I've had so much fun with you. You've made me feel things I didn't know were possible." He grinned and I lowered my gaze. "You also helped me realize that I'm not the monster I thought I was. Even if it has just been a few days, these days with you have been... something."

"Aye, they have been quite amazing. Ye a monster? No way. Anyone who ever could think such nightmarish things obviously never took the time to get to," he tilted my chin up, "know ye. Ye

82

are worth so much, Abby." He leaned in toward me with half hooded lids. "Truly." His lips lightly kissed mine.

My heart fluttered. I cupped his cheeks and broke the kiss. He sighed with a soft growl, which caused me to giggle. "I'm sorry, but I'm not sorry."

"Umm, what?" He furrowed his brows at me.

"Yeah, I think that might be an American saying. What I'm trying to tell you is, thank you. For everything. You've been so... just wow." I shook my head and smiled. "There are no words for how amazing you've been."

He grinned. "Well darling, ye are absolutely worth it." He kissed me quickly then pulled away. "Let's get inside, yeah? I'd like to make you the last meal of the day."

"Oh, that sounds good." We got out of the car and met at the back of it. We intertwined our hands and made our way toward the garage door. Our last meal of the day might be our last meal together. My smile quickly shifted to a frown.

"Now what is it, woman? I thought ye were happy? Do I need to wear ma kilt traditional style for that smile to return?"

"What?" I laughed and shook my head. "No, well not yet anyway. Keep it in mind for later," I winked. "I was just thinking is all."

"Ahh, thinking of me naked, were ye?" He chuckled. "Well, if ye would like me to cook naked..."

"Oh god, Clive, not everything is about me thinking of you naked!" I laughed again. Although the thought of him naked was... well hell, I would love to see him naked, but I have to ask myself. Is it too soon?

It's never stopped you before.

Well, it's different this time. Shut up!

We made it into the house and Douglas immediately greeted us.

"Welcome home, Master Patterson. Miss Masters, as always, it is a pleasure." He bowed slightly.

"Douglas, it is a pleasure seeing you again as well. We're about to have dinner."

"Ahh, I will see to ye later then." Douglas turned and left the room without giving me a second glance... except for a smile.

We made our way into the kitchen. Clive pulled out a few chicken breasts and set them out, then began working on side dishes.

"What can I help with?" I offered. I stood next to him and watched as his cutting knife sliced through potatoes.

"Nothing, love. Just sit over there and continue to look beautiful." He grinned then leaned in and kissed me. Clive was amazing. He had his own business, was a wonderful man, and knew how to cook. Was there anything he couldn't do?

"So," he started, "how long has yer mother been jealous of ye?"

I coughed and then cleared my throat. I wasn't expecting this question, of all questions. "What?"

He glanced over his shoulder at me and smiled. Maybe his way of showing me he's here and not going anywhere? I'm not sure. "It seems yer mother is jealous of whatever ye have over her. I'm asking if ye know why."

I had never thought of my mother being jealous of me. What the hell could she be jealous of? I shook my head. "If it's all the same to you, I would rather not talk about her."

"No problem," he glanced to me again, "how about ye father?"

"Curious about me, are you?" I smiled. Clive nodded then turned back to his cutting board. I sighed and thought about my father. "I'm not sure what there is to tell. He works so much and is hardly home. He's into his work, but I told you that." Clive nodded and I glanced at my hands. Faded scars set as reminders of the fights, the torment from my mother, even the fight I had with Lexi. I sighed.

"He's had an on-again, off-again love affair with his secretary for years. My mother has known about it, but she stayed with

84

him. I don't think my father could bring himself to leave my mother, though."

"Oh? Why's that?"

I shook my head. "I think she's too fragile."

"Is she sick?" Clive grabbed a towel and wiped his hands, then came over to me. He took a seat for a moment and gave me his attention. I wasn't sure what to make of this, other than feeling flattered. I don't recall a time anyone has tried to figure out my family. Then again, I have always pushed them away.

"I guess that depends on your definition of what sick is. She drinks... a lot. She thinks everyone is out to get her. She blames me for everything that has happened to her and everything that happened with my father. Apparently, it is my fault he fucks his secretary. It is my fault the pool boy won't come more than twice a week to see her. It is my fault she drinks and she never, ever lets me forget that I'll never be good enough for anything.

"Did you know she showed up at my modeling agency, the day I was going to be signed to a top modeling contract, and ruined it? She came in drunk and belligerent." I shook my head and recalled that day, as if it had just happened. "She mouthed off that I probably fucked my way up the line, the way I fucked my principal at high school and college to get the best grades. I'll have you know I never did any such thing. Anyway, she threw herself on the agent, who was a man and gay, and tried to make out with him. She wanted to show them she was better than I was. She was removed by force. I was then asked to leave." I shook my head again and stared at nothing. "She ruined everything," I whispered and wiped my eyes.

Clive reached over and grabbed my hands, then gave them a squeeze. "So ye are not ready to talk about yer mother?"

I let out a sound like a huff, mixed with a laugh. "Apparently, I was." I sighed, let go of one of his hands, and wiped my eyes again. "I'm so sorry; I didn't mean to get all dumpy."

He chuckled and watched me for a moment. "I don't think I

know what dumpy means, however, if ye feel better, then I'm happy to be of service." Clive reached up and wiped a tear from my cheek, then cupped my face. "Ye are absolutely beautiful, Abby. Ye deserve so much more than ye have been given."

"I've been given so much already, though," I protested.

"No, ye haven't. Ye may have been given a roof over yer head… and said roof may have been a big one with funding behind it, but that is not ma point. Ma point is, ye have not been given the love and attention a child deserves. It is not fair to ye, and how dare them for holding ye accountable for their misgivings.

"Now ye listen to me, Abby Masters. When ye head back to Texas, because at some point, ye will need to decide where life will lead ye, ignore them. Ignore the insults. Ignore the vices. Ignore everything. Just focus on one thing and one thing only."

I tried so hard to hold a brave face. I learned at young age to hide the emotions so my mother could not use them against me. So my friends could not call me weak. So I could protect myself from being hurt.

"What am I supposed to focus on, Clive?" I asked in a soft voice.

"Me."

I met his gaze and it was intense. "What?"

"Aye, ye heard me woman. We are friends now, yeah?"

I nodded. "I certainly hope so," I told him.

"Good. Then ye always have a place to come back to. The guest room will belong to ye when and if you need it. Good?"

I sighed and shook my head. "You don't have to do that, Clive."

"I know I don't have to do that, love. I'm doing that because I want to."

"Why?" I asked. "I don't deserve your kindness."

"What the hell did I just tell ye earlier? Aye, ye do. Ye will always have a place here at Patterson Manor. Understood?"

"Clive," I began to protest again.

"No, Abby, dammit listen to me! Ye need sanctuary? Ye have it.

Ye need a place to sleep? Ye have it. Ye need to get laid because ye are feeling randy? Dammit, pick me and ye have it."

I grinned and lowered my gaze.

"Understood?" He asked again as he tilted up my head.

I nodded. "Yes, understood."

"Good. Now let me get this dinner cooked. It won't cook itself," he grinned as he stood.

"Did you really just say randy?"

He chuckled. "Would ye rather me say horny?"

I grinned and watched him work in the kitchen.

An hour later, we were stuffed. The chicken was amazing as were his potatoes. Clive led me into his den and a gigantic flat screen television hung on the wall. I stared at it, mouth agape.

"How big is that thing?" I asked.

He chuckled. "Would ye like to find out?"

"What?" I turned to him and found an amused expression on his face. I laughed and shook my head. "Maybe later?"

"Ooh, promise?" He asked and waggled his brows. He pulled me close and wrapped his arms around my body. He was so strong and I felt protected in his embrace. I grinned then shrugged playfully.

"Only if you're a good boy, Clive."

"Fuck me," he whispered. "I didn't expect ye to call me on ma bluff." I laughed and rested my cheek on his chest. "Oh right, television. It is a 94-inch flat screen.

"Holy hell! Why so big?" I asked. "I mean, it's nice to have but so big?"

"Aye, there's nothing like watching people fuck on a big screen."

"Oh my god! You're a perv!" I laughed and pulled away, then playfully slapped his arm.

He chuckled. "It allows me to watch multiple stations at once. The naked fucking is nice, also."

"That leaves something to be desired, I'm sure," I retorted.

"Want to test that theory?"

"Oh, umm… are you serious?"

He nodded. Clive pressed a few buttons on the oversized remote he was holding and I heard locks sound.

"What did you do?" I asked. I knew I sounded a little alarmed, but I'd had a means of escape through a few doors… now I had none. "Clive, did you lock me inside?"

"Abby," he said in a lowered tone, "ye are safe here, I promise ye that. Nothing will happen that ye don't want to happen. I'll unlock them now if ye want."

I could see the hurt in his eyes. I wasn't sure how I felt about being locked inside a room with anyone. I'd always looked for the quickest exit, assuming it was needed. Now? Well, rather than panicking, I sighed and stepped toward Clive.

"No, it's okay," I laid my hand across his wrist, "I promise, it's okay. It was unexpected, but I promise, it is fine."

"Positive?"

I nodded.

"All right, then." He turned the remote toward me and pointed at a few buttons, then explained what each one unlocked. I watched him, appreciating what he was doing. I took the remote in my hands and set it down. I pressed my palms on his chest and stepped closer.

"Thank you," I whispered before I rose up on my toes and kissed him.

11

*H*e mumbled against my lips, "Ye are so beautiful, woman." His hands moved to my waist and slipped around my back. He pulled me closer until our bodies were flush. His strong hands moved over my ass and he squeezed it, pulling me that much closer against his body.

I'd never wanted a naked body against my own as much as I wanted Clive's… right now.

I tilted back slightly as he leaned into me. I held onto his neck as our kissing turned more heated. My tongue glided over his lips and he growled. The sound sent a shiver through me. I wanted him to do it again.

Clive began to push against me until I walked backwards. I only stopped when the couch in the room met the back of my legs.

I lowered myself, as did Clive. He pulled away long enough to catch his breath. "Abby, please tell me if I go too far, woman. You have me rock hard!" His gaze met mine. He held me at that moment and I could not move; I could not breathe. I wanted Clive as much as he wanted me… if not more.

"I want you," I whispered, "very much so."

He grinned and captured my lips again. After a moment, he pulled away to ask, "So, porn, yeah?"

I laughed and shook my head. "Porn, no. Music? Maybe. We need something in here for the silence."

"Oh, the silence won't be an issue here shortly." Clive moved to my neck and devoured me. I sighed with pleasure and my head tilted to give him more access. He sucked lightly on my lobe and his breath lightly touched my ear. The feeling sent shivers down my body. "Ye are so beautiful, Abby," he whispered

I gripped his biceps and my breath heaved slightly. His hand moved to my breast and he squeezed softly. My nipples responded immediately to his touch. My bra was thin so I knew he felt it, if the growl he emitted was any indication.

He tugged at my top. I lifted my arms above my head and pulled it off, then tossed it. I lay back against the couch and watched him watching me. His eyes scanned my body with appreciation. His lips occasionally would lift in the corner, giving away a hint of a grin. His eyes... Clive had this intense gaze that took my breath away.

He reached for my neck and lightly ran his fingers down the length of it until he reached the décolleté of my bra. The tips of his fingers traced the lining of my left breast first. Once he reached the peak of my nipple, he traced it lightly. My nipple responded immediately by growing hard. Clive's gaze intensified slightly.

He then shifted to my right breast and made the same movement. I closed my eyes and sighed. He kissed between my breasts and a hand slipped behind my back. Unclasping my bra, he slowly slid it down my arms. When he lifted, he smiled softly.

"Beautiful," he whispered. Clive grasped both of my breasts, squeezed them slightly, and pressed them together. He leaned in and took both nipples into his mouth, one at a time.

My fingers moved into his hair. It was soft and it curled slightly. I adjusted one of my legs and moved it to the outside of his body. Clive moved his body until he was positioned between my legs.

He grasped one of my legs, behind the knee, and pulled it up. He returned his lips to mine and pressed his hips against me. When he rubbed against me, I moaned against his lips.

"Ye like that, baby?" He asked. He gripped my chin and lifted my neck to the side. He kissed along my sensitive skin and pushed against me again. "I asked ye a question, love. Do ye like that?"

"Oh my god, yes." My arms slipped around his lower back and I tugged at his shirt. I felt his skin against my hands and I could not get him naked fast enough. My breath was coming faster and my panties were wet, so wet.

Clive sat up and pulled his shirt off. His naked torso was beautiful. My fingers skimmed along his chest and strong abs. He had a tuft of red hair in the center of his chest. I wanted to lick him, run my tongue across the dips in his skin where the muscle line contoured. I glanced down at the outline of his erection. Hell, I wanted to run my tongue along the length of his cock. If the outline was any indication, he was huge!

I met his gaze and he smirked. "I'm going to get ye naked, woman. Are ye okay with me doing that?"

I smiled. "Oh sugar, I'm okay with just about anything right now." That was absolutely the truth. I wanted this; so did he. Oh my god, did I want this.

He chuckled and reached for my pants. "Sugar?" He shook his head with a grin and unbuttoned my pants, then tugged them down my legs. My red panties, which matched my red bra, were the only item that remained on my body. He tugged off my shoes and pants then looked over my body with admiration.

"Fuck me, woman, ye been hiding this under all yer clothes for this long?" He shook his head and laid a hand across his mouth. "I should punish ye for such bodily abuse. A body like this needs to be exposed." He leaned down and kissed between my breasts. He squeezed them together against his face. "Needs to be kissed." He kissed along my stomach to my waist. I grinned as I tried not to giggle. I was still ticklish. He made his way back to my navel and kissed it.

His hands moved down my body to my legs. He moved a finger into the seam of my panties, between my thighs. I gasped. He watched me for a moment and I nodded, showing him it was okay.

He lightly ran his finger against my folds. I bit my lip and watched him. He touched me lightly then his thumb pressed against my clit. I gasped again and closed my eyes. Clive removed his finger. I opened my eyes and found him watching me. I smiled. He hooked fingers into either side of my panties then tugged them down my legs slowly.

"A body this beautiful needs to be tasted." He leaned in and kissed against my folds. My breath caught in my chest and I laid my head back.

"Oh god," I whispered and closed my eyes. I felt the couch move and when I opened my eyes, he had positioned his face between my legs. Clive looked up and smiled.

"I want to taste you," he said with a growl. Before I could say anything, he lowered his head and I gasped when his tongue slipped between my folds.

My heartbeat raced. My breathing turned to panting, which eventually became loud as I moaned. My back arched from the lashing his tongue gave my clit. He slipped a finger inside me and I let out a louder moan. He growled against me. The vibrations caused my hips to buck.

"Oh my god, Clive!"

He growled again. I've never had an orgasm during oral sex. Apparently, when others had done it, they had been doing it wrong because with Clive, without a doubt, he was going to make me cum.

I raised my head to watch him and in that same moment, he glanced up at me. He held my gaze as he continued his ministrations. This was the most erotic thing I had ever done.

I moaned and laid my head back again. I reached for him and grabbed his hair. I pulled him closer and he growled hard into my pussy.

"Clive! Oh shit!" I moved my body against his mouth as I felt my orgasm building. He inserted another finger and pumped. He sucked on my clit and watched me. Like a wave hitting the ocean, I came... hard. I yelled out and my hips bucked. "Clive!"

He pulled back and watched me for a moment. My chest rose and fell with the heavy breaths I was taking.

"Woman, are ye all right?" He grinned and I nodded. His face was wet, at least until he wiped his hand down his mouth and chin.

Without wasting any time, Clive quickly pushed his pants and boxer briefs off his body. I reached for him and pulled him down to me. Our lips crashed into one another's. I could taste myself on him. I kissed him harder. His cock rubbed against my pussy and I began to move my hips against him.

"Are ye ready for this?" he whispered.

I nodded. "Fuck yes."

"That's ma girl," he said with a heated tone. He reached between us and lined up his head, then pushed.

I gasped and held onto him. He held still inside me for a moment, allowing me to adjust to his size. He kissed me softly and whispered to me, "Ye are so beautiful."

When I was ready, I began moving my body underneath his. Clive pulled back and pushed again. I moaned against his neck then I kissed his ear. "Oh my god, Clive," I whispered.

"Aye, fuck, love," he growled, "oh fuck!" He picked up his rhythm and kissed along my jawline. The man was a God, purely.

Clive sat up and back on his heels. He grabbed my hips and pulled my body up to his. He began to thrust against me and I reached above my head for some real estate, anything to hold onto. Finding the end of the couch, I grasped it hard and Clive's thrusts became more... just more.

He growled and his eyes roamed over my body. He focused on the movement of my breasts. His teeth gritted and he groaned hard. "Woman, I'm going to cum, ye hear me?"

I nodded and held tighter onto the couch. "Harder," I whispered.

"What was that?" he asked as he slowed his rhythm down. "Did ye ask me to fuck ye... harder?"

I opened my eyes and bit my lip. Had I taken it too far? Did he like it when I asked him to do it harder? My heart skipped in its rhythm and I boldly nodded. "Yes. Harder," I said with determination.

"That's what I thought ye said." He grinned and his grip tightened on my hips. Clive did not disappoint. His body thrust against mine... hard. My voice carried throughout the room as I yelled out. Between a moan and yelling his name, Clive was making me cum again.

"Oh yes," I yelled out, "yes!"

"Mmm, that's ma girl." He grinned and as I watched him, he closed his eyes. His face hardened slightly and his lips parted. He gasped and suddenly he thrust once, twice. He sighed with a groan and his head tilted back. "Fuck me, Abby!"

I grinned and released the couch. My fingers skimmed his abs as Clive released my hips. He pulled out and lay down next to me. His arm wrapped around my waist and he pulled me close. My right leg laid over his and I rested my head in the crook of his shoulder.

"So, I'll take it was good for ye?" He asked me.

I grinned and playfully shrugged. "It was all right." I felt him move underneath me. He lifted his brows in surprise.

"Just... all right? Just all right? Ye are killing me, woman!"

I giggled and kissed his lips. "You were amazing, Clive. You know you were."

He settled down into the couch and lifted his free arm under his head. "I'm so good, I should yell ma own name." I laughed and he turned to gaze at me. "What? Ye know it's true."

I nodded and patted his chest. "You were amazing, dear. Absolutely amazing."

～

*A*t some point, I fell asleep in Clive's arms. It was a nice place to fall asleep. I felt safe and warm. I was also naked. His arm was around my shoulders and he was still sleeping. He snored softly and his eyes were moving about under his lids.

What was he dreaming about? Me? His bar? Past loves?

I didn't want to think about past loves. My track record was seriously black. The closest I had to a relationship was... Blaine. I rolled my eyes at the thought of him. I was nothing more than a fuck toy to him. I knew that now.

I think a part of me always knew this, but knowing and admitting? Two different things.

A sigh left my lips as I slowly sat up. I stretched and glanced over my shoulder at the sleeping body next to me. Good god, he was sexy and strong. I wondered what he did for fun outside his bar. I wondered what his relationship was like with his parents and siblings. He said they were close.

I glanced down at my bare feet. The shiny red polish seemed to stare back, judging me. My head relaxed and I rested my elbows on my knees. I had just slept with a man I knew nothing about.

He had a bar connected to a distillery he runs.

He was Scottish.

He was wealthy.

He had a lot of cars.

Was there anything else? I'm sure there was, but what? I sighed and rose from the couch and collected my undergarments. I had no concept of time and had no idea how long we had been asleep.

When I reached one of the curtained windows in the room, I pulled it aside and prepared to squint from the sun. I was surprised at the opposite. The sun had descended and the sky was full of evening stars.

"What time is it?" I whispered to myself. Right then my stomach growled. I glanced over at the couch and Clive was still asleep. I released the curtain and pulled on my panties, then my bra. I wasn't sure if one of the pull ropes was in this room, or if Douglas would attempt to come this way with Clive and I holed up in here. I needed to get home. I felt my eyes sting as tears threatened. I made a point to find myself on this trip and what happened? I found myself in someone's bed instead.

Nothing with me had changed.

Nothing.

"Abby?"

Damn, he was awake. I quickly wiped my eyes and sucked in a deep breath, then exhaled. I slowly turned to face my latest conquest.

Clive rose from the couch and his naked body was in full view. I couldn't look at him. I felt ashamed. I closed my eyes and lowered my head.

"Abby," he whispered, "what's the matter? Was I that bad that ye need to cry about it?"

He was attempting to humor me. I offered a slight grin then shook my head. "No, you were amazing." He touched my chin and lifted my face up.

"Tell me what is wrong then?" His eyes were full of concern. He lightly traced my cheek.

"The intent of this trip," I closed my eyes and took a step back from him, "was for me to find myself. I needed to get away from my family, from everything back home. I had not planned to sleep with anyone, jump in anyone's bed, and I certainly didn't expect to meet you."

He raised a single brow. "Are ye telling me ye regret what we did and us meeting?"

"What? Oh, gosh, no! Not at all! No, that's not what I mean. I'm sorry. Clive, you're wonderful. You deserve so much better... so much more than what I can offer you, what I am. Please, just let me go home."

"No, I'm afraid I can't do that."

I looked up at this and held his gaze. I thought maybe he was teasing but the look in his eyes indicated he was serious. "What do you mean?"

"What I mean is, no. Ye are not going anywhere. Ye did nothing wrong here, Abby. I still want you." He closed the distance between us and cupped my face. "What ye don't understand, lass, is that they don't deserve ye. None of them do. If they can't see what I see in ye, then they're the stubborn fools."

I hiccupped and did my best to stop from crying. I hated being a girl sometimes. I nodded and reached for his hands. I removed them from my face and lowered them to my sides. "Thank you," I whispered.

"Honestly, woman, ye need to speak up. I can barely hear ye."

I grinned and met his gaze. He was smiling and it was absolutely sincere. "Thank you," I said a little louder.

"Now, if ye are ready to head back, I'll be happy to take ye, but not before I feed ye. I heard something rumble earlier when I was over there."

My eyes widened slightly. "Oh my gosh," I lowered my gaze and felt my skin turn hot from the blush.

He chuckled. "Now if ye wait here, I'll grab ye something to drink and some food, aye?"

I nodded and lifted my gaze slowly to his. He smiled and stepped closer. He cupped my face again and tilted my head up. "Ye are amazing, woman. Never underestimate yerself." I nodded again. He leaned in and kissed me.

12

a few days passed after Clive and I slept together. At night, either he came to my hotel or I went to his house. It is Friday and my plane leaves Sunday. He asked me not to tell him when I'm going. How was I supposed to do this? How did I up and leave a man I've met and developed feelings for?

You come back for him, idiot.

Shut up.

I sighed and pulled on a pair of strappy sandals. Clive said he wanted to take me to a game of Shinty. I had never heard of this and was curious what to wear. I'm assuming it is something outdoors. I nodded and smiled, as if to go along with the idea.

A knock at my door sounded. Clive was here. I sighed and grabbed my purse. I looked out the peep hole of the door and could not see out. He had covered it with his finger.

Clever. Real clever.

"Let go of the hole, Clive," I ordered.

He chuckled. "I would rather not, if it is all the same to ye." He released it. He winked at me and grinned. He was wearing a light blue jersey with the number 16 stitched to it.

Curious, I opened the door. He had on a pair of black shorts and blue and black wide striped socks. I grinned and my brows rose. "Well, don't you look… dashing."

He growled and pushed his way into my hotel room. I giggled and he pressed me against the wall as the door shut. He kissed me and his hands moved down to my ass. He lifted me and wrapped my legs around his waist.

"I would be happy to fuck ye now, if we had the time, but alas," he continued to kiss me, "we need to go."

"I'll hold you to it tonight, then."

He sighed against my lips and lightly pressed his forehead to mine. "You drive me insane, woman. Ye know that, aye?"

I nodded. Absolutely I knew that. He did the same for me. Clive was so intense and gave everything he had. He didn't hold back. Many could take note from this man, including me.

"Can you please tell me a little about this shitty game?"

"Shitty?" He pulled back and stared into my eyes. "I promise ye, love, Shinty is not shitty."

"Oh god," I pressed my fingers lightly to my lips. "That was a slip on my part. I'm so sorry!"

He chuckled and shook his head. "It was quite funny, but don't knock the game, love. Shinty is like ground hockey. Hockey is on ice whereas Shinty is on grass."

I nodded. "Okay, I can follow that. I've been to a few hockey games before. The *Dallas Stars* aren't too bad."

He shrugged. "I don't follow hockey. Too cold." He grinned. "Ye ready?"

"Sure am. Your friends know I'm coming?" I smiled.

"Aye, and they're looking forward to meeting ye. Scarlet has the day off. She's involved with one of the guys. I'm sure she'll be happy to have a friendly female face there."

"Oh? Why is that?"

"Well, love, we really get into the game. She usually doesn't come, but since ye will be there, she changed her mind." I smiled to this.

The drive over took us about a good hour. The sky was still clear, save for a few streaks of thin clouds. I opened my car door and stepped out. The area was wide open and surrounded by trees. The grass was so green. A part of me wanted to lie down and roll in it, like a child; the other wanted to explore the woods.

"Abby!" Scarlet's voice echoed through the open area. I smiled when I saw my new friend. She pulled me in a hug and squeezed. "I'm so glad ye came!" She had on red blouse that complemented her black hair.

"So, who's your man and is he on the same team?"

"Jacob is ma guy," she pointed to a young man across the field also wearing red. Jacob was tall like Clive. I could not tell right away what his hair color was as he had recently taken clippers to his scalp. He was thick like Clive though. They all were.

My question about the teams was quickly answered when Jacob turned and I saw 21 on his jersey. Blue against red. Scarlet was also wearing red. I looked down to my light yellow top.

"Why didn't you tell me to wear blue?" I asked Clive.

"Ye would've done that for me?" he asked with a grin. I nodded. He leaned in and kissed me. "I'll remember that for next time." He kissed me again then took off toward the field in a light jog.

Next time.

I sighed and looped my arm through Scarlet's. Most likely, there wouldn't be a next time. At least not for a while.

"What's on yer mind, Abby?" Scarlet asked me. I smiled and looked her way, then shook my head.

"Nothing to worry yourself about. Let's enjoy the game, shall we?"

"Absolutely. I brought chairs out with me. I wasn't sure if ye would have one or not."

"Thank you," I told her as I took a seat. "So, is it customary for us to sit together as we are cheering for two different teams?"

"Cheering?" Scarlet asked me with a tilt in her head.

I nodded. "Cheering for your team. You know, go team, and stuff."

"Oh, cheer," she repeated and nodded a few times. "Aye, I got ya now."

"So do you stand and scream for Jacob's team?"

"Why would I do that?" She asked me with a curious expression.

"Do you not support your man in the game?"

"Oh, I do, but not by yelling at him to do better. He does just fine."

I grinned. "All right, then. What do you do while the game is going?"

"Usually it is between me calling him an ass for missing the ball or yelling at the other team, like Clive, that he's a donkey."

I laughed. "Isn't donkey and ass the same thing?"

She winked. "Depends on who ye are calling the ass."

The game went on. The men hit the ball and lunged into one another. A few times, the sticks would be taken to the knees, causing the opponent to fall backwards. This happened to Clive once. I rose to my feet and watched in concern.

"Sit down, would ye?" Scarlet asked. "He doesn't need a nurse."

"What if it was Jacob?"

"What if it was? He'd get up and go after the ass who did it."

"For a fight?" I asked with concern.

She laughed and shook her head. "No, to return the favor!"

The thin streaks of clouds had grown since we arrived. The air had grown heavy with humidity and the wind began to pick up. It felt like rain and I didn't have my umbrella. At least I wasn't wearing white. I glanced down at my light yellow shirt. I might as well be though. I sighed and continued to watch the game.

Something had just happened because Clive's team is cheering. I glanced to Scarlet and she shook her head. "YE POMPOUS ASSHOLE! YE SERIOUSLY LET HIM SCORE?"

Jacob lifted his arms to his side, as if to say what gives?

I giggled and covered my lips with my fingers. "So, you don't cheer but you will yell? Ahh, okay."

"Shut it," she told me. I grinned and crossed my legs. Clive had thrust his arms into the air. It looked like he'd made the shot and from the looks of it, the winning shot. I smiled a little more.

We made eye contact and he waved at me. I pumped the air slightly with my fist and smiled. *Well done*, I mouthed. He blew an air kiss to me.

"Oh stop it; I will vomit!" Scarlet rolled her eyes and rose from her chair. She began walking onto the field toward Jacob. He frowned at her and she shook her head. Suddenly, Scarlet jumped into his arms and wrapped her legs around his waist, then kissed him.

I felt like I was spying in on something intimate and looked away. I met Clive's gaze as he headed in my direction. Oh boy, he was hot and sweaty... holy shit, he was hot! His clothes clung to him and his hair was wet, causing it to curl.

He reached my chair as I stood. Without hesitating, he pulled me close and kissed me. The man smelled of deodorant, cologne, and sweat... and I wanted him.

"Did ye have a good time?" he asked in a husky voice. I nodded and slipped my arms around his neck. He was sweaty but I didn't mind.

"I sure did. Scarlet is quite pissed though."

He shrugged. "She'll mend his pride and be over it soon enough."

The wind blew a little harder and the clouds rumbled.

"We should go soon," I told him.

"Why? Because of a little rain?" he shook his head with a smile. "It's good luck if it rains after a game."

"Is it?" I asked with a smile.

He shrugged. "Dunno, just made that up." He winked and I laughed. It thundered again and it was closer. A few drops hit my shoulders and I stepped closer to Clive. "Are ye scared of the rain, love?" He lowered his voice and it had a seductive charm to it.

I shook my head no. "But if I say yes, will you protect me?"

"Aye, with ma dying breath," he breathed as he kissed me. Right then, the sky opened up and the downpour started. I yelled out and pulled Clive closer to me. My clothes were soaked quickly. He chuckled.

"Ahh, now this, *this* is how to enjoy life!" He laughed and looked up at the sky. The rain washed down his face and he opened his mouth, allowing it inside.

I laughed and pressed my forehead against his chest. The rain continued to pound against us and in that moment, I did not care in the least.

$\sim$

*W*e made it back to my hotel. Clive had a packed bag with him and brought it up. We received a few stares and curious gazes from people staying at the hotel. He shrugged them off and pulled me close.

I opened the door to my room and we walked inside. The temperature was where I liked it: cold. Right now, however, it was too much with our wet clothes.

"Oh my gosh, I have to get out of these clothes!" I glanced down and found my nipples were completely erect. I also saw Clive noticed that as well.

"Aye," he said in his husky voice. He pulled his blue shirt off and let it drop to the floor in a plop. His chest was wet, as were his abs. I bit my lip and could not move.

Clive grinned and took a step toward me. "Get naked, woman. I'm going to fuck ye in the shower." He reached for me and lightly touched my nipples. My body trembled slightly. I am not sure if it was due to the coldness in the room or Clive's touch.

I reached for my shirt and began to pull it off my body, when it decided, at this moment, to lodge itself. I pulled and couldn't get it off. "Will you help me?"

His warmth was close. I felt his fingers touch my bare sides. Chills moved up my skin as he lightly ran his touch over my body. Then I giggled. "Are ye ticklish?" He suddenly started tickling me and I screamed.

"OH MY GOD! YOU STOP! STOP! STOP IT!" I laughed so hard I started to fall backwards. Thankfully, the wall behind me kept me from falling down, that and Clive's arms around my body.

His lips kissed on my abs then his hands moved to my back. His fingers gripped into my skin and I gasped. I had temporarily forgotten my shirt was stuck. Clive took a hold of the garment and untangled it, then pulled it off.

His face... he was so serious and seductive. He lightly touched my cheek then pressed the other hand against the wall, next to my head. He kissed me softly on the lips.

I reached for his shorts and pushed them over his hips. He kicked them off, along with his shoes. Clive unbuttoned my shorts and I shimmied out of the wet garments. He knelt down to help me step out of them then glanced up my body.

"Ye are a goddess, woman. Absolute goddess!" He kissed my thigh then kissed against the mound of my sex. He began to rise and kissed my abs to my breasts, neck, and finally, my lips.

I mumbled against his lips, "Shower?"

He nodded. "Aye, and fucking."

"Oh god," I whispered.

*T*he day had finally arrived. I had not rushed for it, nor prayed for it to arrive, but it had. I glanced at my ticket in hand for India. I felt my eyes burn slightly as they became wet. Nick, my trusty cab driver, took me to the airport that morning. Clive had left earlier to tend to his distillery before the bar opened.

Don't tell me good-bye. Just go, it'll be easier that way.

I sighed and dropped my gaze as I entered into the airport security area. I set my belongings on the conveyor and removed my shoes. I stepped through the scanner successfully then pulled my shoes back on my feet. I hated this part of traveling. Some people came in flip-flops. How could they stand the dirty floor?

I grabbed my things and headed toward my gate. An open seat by the runway tunnel sat empty and I took it. I pulled my phone from my purse and saw my light flashing from a message.

Closing my eyes, I swiped my finger across the screen and saw it was from Clive. With a shaky finger, I opened and found a selfie of him, giving me that seductive look he gives. Unbeknownst to him, Scarlet was in the background, photo bombing him. I giggled and looked to my left and right and figured, no one knew me, what the hell?

I held my camera out and took a selfie with the plane behind me.

See you soon.

I pressed send then immediately turned off my phone. I couldn't talk to him if he called. I could not hear the sound of his voice and still leave. I needed to do this, for me, for us, for any future I might have with him. I sighed and shoved my phone back in my purse.

The flight attendant began talking through the speaker and announced our flight to New Delhi. "Now boarding rows one through ten, rows one through ten." I sighed, picked up my luggage, and stepped through the long walk toward the plane. I felt like I was walking *The Green Mile*, so to speak. I was leaving behind an amazing man to continue my exploration of the world... and of myself.

He would be back in Scotland, waiting for my return. He would be. He had to be. I hoped he would wait for me. I told him a few nights ago when I finished my trip to India that I would return to Scotland. I had another flight to Australia but right now, I wanted Scotland more than anything else. I wanted him... no, I needed him.

I stuffed my belongings into my overhead compartment and took my seat in first class. I had a sleeper style seat. I didn't imagine I'd meet someone like Clive on this flight. There was no one like him. That thought had me smiling.

She likes the whipped cream. She likes to lick if off my body.

I grinned wider at the memory of our first meeting. Soon enough, the plane would take off. Then, I would be in India. Not soon enough, I would be returning to Scotland and into the arms of the amazing man I've grown feelings for.

In the past, landing the man I was after ended the game for me. I wanted something I couldn't have but once I had it, I was done.

Now, with Clive, it was different. He was definitely not a game and not someone to be toyed with. He was... He was something else entirely. What that was right now, I'm not sure, but I was happy to spend time finding out.

~

*A*fter landing, I retrieved my luggage and went outside. The air was thick, almost like it was filled with pollution. I looked around and saw I stuck out like a sore thumb. I was blond, tall, and thin. The majority of the people here was medium size, and covered in clothes that were unfamiliar to me. Their hair, their eyes, everything about them were dark.

I felt nervous as I approached a waiting cab. The man inside glanced up with a double take.

"American?"

I nodded with a smile. "I'm staying at the Le Méridien."

He grinned and started the car. He opened the trunk for me, then after putting my bag inside, we took off. I sank into the back seat slightly. I didn't bother looking to the driver's name. I don't think I would be calling on him like I had Nick.

I sighed and thought of my temporary driver, Scotland, and my Clive. Glancing out the window, I saw the city of New Delhi pass by. It was beautiful and busy! So many people were either walking or riding bikes. It was almost too much to take in. I'm not much of a crowd type person. It was possible that I would have an anxiety attack.

We arrived at the Le Méridien. I paid the driver and he helped me retrieve my bags from the trunk. The bell staff came up soon after and helped me inside. I checked in and received my room key.

I felt like I was on auto pilot. The bell staff helped me to my room and offered to hang my clothes up for me. I shook my head and thanked them. I considered offering a tip then remembered what happened in Scotland.

"May I tip you for helping me today?"

The young man named Abu nodded. "Yes, madam, thank you." He bowed slightly. I offered him ten American dollars. He smiled and bowed again. "If you need anything," he offered, "please call me."

I unpacked and pulled out my travel guide. I saw a few signs at the airport for Ashrams that offered meditation yoga, spiritual lifting, and guidance. I wondered if it was an all stop shop for yoga. Finding one in my guide, I picked up the hotel room phone and called the number.

An unfamiliar dialect in a male's voice answered the phone. "*Hailo, Āśrama.*"

I cleared my throat. "Hello there. Do you speak English?"

"Ahh, yes, madam. How may I be of service?" the man asked me.

I explained I wanted to visit his Ashram. He asked me a few questions regarding my potential visit and I considered telling him I wanted to find spiritual guidance. I decided against it. I wrote down the information and said my good byes.

I wanted, more than anything, to put my past behind me. I didn't want to be the person I had become. I didn't want to become... my mother. I sighed and lay back on my bed, then stared at the ceiling.

What now? I thought to myself. I could set up my laptop and check out the area.

You could send a message to Clive, let him know you're here.

Yeah, I could, but was I hanging onto something that might not be mine to hang onto?

I closed my eyes and inhaled deeply, then slowly released it. I'm completely on my own, again. My mother's words were a distant memory and my father might not have realized I had even left. Since he was never home, there was a good chance he didn't know. It's not like my mother ever told him anything.

I sat up and headed for my laptop, setting it up on the desk provided in my room. When I turned it on, the image of me and my friends... well, maybe former friends... stared back at me. I clicked on the internet icon and *Google* stared back at me. After inputting my WiFi password, I wrote down the closest *Starbucks*, a few bookstores and the address to the Ashram.

After clicking another tab, I pulled up my email. I knew I should check in with my parents... caring or not, at least give them some piece of mind that I was still alive and okay, and I did just that. I pulled my purse close and reached inside for my chap stick. My lips felt dry and when I felt a card, I pulled it out. Not only were my lips dry, now my mouth was, too.

Patterson Distillery – Owner and Proprietor Clive Patterson

My thumb absently glided over the embossed name. I had received his card before my first visit to Hitter's Bar and realizing Clive was indeed the owner of both. I recalled how I felt, the idiocy of our interaction and the morning after. The strength of his back, his tattoo, and then I smiled. The memory of how he froze when he thought a spider was crawling on him.

I composed a new message and entered his email into the TO line.

Hello, Clive.
I made it safely to India. The air climate here is quite different from that in Scotland. I already miss your smile and the laughter we shared. Please tell Scarlet I said hello. You have my number if you would like to call.
Bye, for now.
Love, Abby

I stared at the message for a few minutes then hit send. I

closed the top and stood, then decided it was as good as a time as any to head outside. I wanted to visit the Ashram. I had heard good things about the positive growth and self-healing from the yoga performed. Not necessarily the yoga itself, but the meditation involved more specifically. I needed something positive and getting away from Texas had definitely been a good start.

Now was time for locking up the past and looking toward my future. Whether that held Clive or not, time would tell. I would be here long enough to learn about this meditation then I would whisk away to Australia. Who knew what was waiting for me there. I couldn't help the laugh that erupted. I could only picture *Crocodile Dundee*, an eighties movie I'd watched with my friends. I didn't imagine someone like Mic Dundee actually existed, but I guess time would tell. Then again, I had met a Scottish man who made a kilt look incredibly sexy. I could very well end up back there instead. I supposed, at this point, anything was possible.

14

*T*ime passed quickly after arriving in India. Clive emailed and called me a few times. His bar and distillery kept him very busy. I kept myself busy with my touring of India and the Ashram.

Meditation was something I had never tried before India. The first few times were difficult for me to understand. I would close my eyes and my mind would suddenly run rampant with thoughts. Sometimes they were of Clive, other times of my family.

"Inhale deeply, then slowly exhale. Focus on your toes and imagine them not moving. Slowly, move up your body until everything is perfectly still. Then, allow yourself to escape into your mind." The tall, slender man in the Ashram was very patient with me... the tall blonde woman who stood out amongst the other Indian women.

I felt out of place in the beginning, then as time moved forward, the uneasiness began to ease. Soon, some would smile at me, welcoming me into the Ashram. Others continued to ignore me completely. The older man who ran the yoga studio and meditation cycles always welcomed me with nothing more than a nod.

He was thin in build and muscular. His head was shaved...

possibly just completely bald, and he usually wore a tattered red t-shirt and khaki shorts. Barefoot, he would walk through the room and check postures. A few times, he would help me out then make his way to someone else.

One afternoon, I attempted a conversation with him. He made no time to chat on a friendly level. He was a business man only. If I wanted someone to share my thoughts with, I suppose seeking out counsel was my only option.

I didn't blame him, I guess. Hell, I wouldn't want to hear my stories either. A girl with serious parental issues... well, at least I did have parental issues. Now? I'm not so sure. I hadn't thought of them too often since I'd been away from Texas.

Deciding to head back toward my hotel, I noticed festivity going on just down the way. It appeared the streets were blocked off. When my cab pulled to a stop, I leaned forward and asked, "What is going on up ahead?"

"Oh, it is the festival of Diwali!" the driver told me excitedly. He turned around slightly and accepted the cab fare. "Are you familiar, madam?"

I shook my head. "Afraid not. I'm sorry," I offered with a smile.

"Well, then, you should go experience it and enjoy the atmosphere. I guarantee you will not be disappointed." The man smiled and nodded a few times. "Please, go, please!"

"Okay," I told him with a smile. I stepped out of the cab and held onto the door for a moment, then slowly closed it. The driver pulled away as I stepped up onto the curb.

"Diwali," I mumbled under my breath. I took a few steps forward and continued to stare down into the blocked streets. People were walking, some were hugging, and others were trading what looked to be goods.

A few people passed me on the street and they smiled in my direction.

"Excuse me," I asked and one of them turned around, a young

girl maybe sixteen years old. "May I ask what the festival of Diwali is about?"

She smiled and came back to me. She was youthful, short, and slender. A few golden bangles held her long black hair back; she had a small purple stone in the center of her forehead that was attached to a headpiece that lay across her hairline.

The girl reached for my arms and slipped hers through it. "American?" Her accent was strong, but understandable. I nodded a few times with a smile. "Ahh, okay. So Diwali is the festival of lights! We come together to celebrate the victory of light over darkness, knowledge over ignorance, good over evil, and hope over despair." She then appeared to glance over my clothes and raised a brow. "Do you have anything, possibly new or dressier to wear tonight?"

"Umm, I'm sure I do, why, may I ask?" I was curious about this. This culture celebrated everything that was good and pure, from what it sounded like, yet I needed to dress up for this?

"We like to dress in our best clothes to celebrate Diwali and," she looked toward the crowd, "with the exchange happening now, it appears the prayer to Lakshmi is completed."

I blinked. "Lack shmee?" I tried to repeat what she had told me. The girl smiled and shook her head.

"Lakshmi, she is the goddess of wealth and prosperity. Fireworks should be going off at sunset!" She pulled me along toward the crowd.

"I don't have traditional Indian wear, just American, should I find something more traditional?"

She shook her hand at me then her head did a sort of bobble dance. "Not necessary. If you like, we can dress and decorate you for the festival."

"Decorate me?" I asked. She nodded and pulled me along.

"Come, you'll see! Oh, my name is Raksha."

"Hello, my name is Abby."

Raksha pulled me toward the closed barricaded street. Apparently, she had many friends at this party. She was greeted warmly, kissed on her cheek, and conversation that went completely over my head was exchanged.

The conversation had apparently shifted to me when a few of her acquaintances turned to face me. One of them took my hands and held my arms out. She nodded and spoke to Raksha.

"Umm, Raksha, what is happening?" I asked and casually bit my lip. I felt a bit nervous as the women who surrounded us busied themselves with fabrics and shiny objects that looked similar to what they were wearing.

She cleared her throat then leaned in with a lowered voice. "You will be dressed soon, then decorated."

"Against my will?" I asked. I tried to smile, but I'm sure it looked forced. I knew I sounded like I was alarmed, and a part of me was. I had no idea who these people were and I felt like I was walking into a religious event. Maybe I should walk back out.

Raksha giggled to herself. "Of course not! You will remove your clothes and we will dress you, but only if you agree to it." She winked, "Trust me. All is well, American Abby."

I felt myself blush slightly as I grinned. "Just Abby."

Raksha turned to the crew of ladies surrounding us and gave what sounded like instruction, but I could not be certain. I stood still with my fingers intertwined in front of me. I had a chance to look around where we were for about five seconds before someone grabbed a hand and tugged.

"Calō!" She repeated herself and tugged again.

"Umm, Raksha?" I asked and looked at the girl I had just met.

She grinned. "It is okay. This is Amna. She is a friend. She's telling you to come on. Go, it's okay, follow her."

I nodded and glanced back to Amna. "Okay."

I was pulled toward what appeared to be a changing area. It reminded me of the changing huts on the beaches back home in Texas. I stepped inside with the woman and the folds to the entrance closed. The room was very dark, at least until Amna opened one of the... windows? I wasn't sure what it would be called, but when she opened the flap, bright sunshine poured inside.

She mumbled something to me in her language that I did not understand. I shook my head with a smile, hoping she knew I had no idea what she was saying. She then held her arms up in the air, signifying I needed to disrobe.

I sighed and closed my eyes. "Jesus, help me." I gave a silent prayer that I would not be humiliated and jailed for indecent exposure in front of a woman I had just met.

After I removed my top, I held my arms over my body, regardless that my bra was still on. Amna picked up a bright pink garment and walked toward me. She draped it over my shoulders then set to work on weaving it around my body. She tapped my arms a few times to move them, and I obeyed. She then tightened the top of the garment and stepped back. She nodded once to herself then grabbed the matching bottom piece.

"Mō a," she spoke to me again and I shook my head. She motioned over her bottom area by patting her hips and bottom. I nodded in understanding.

I set to remove my shorts then set them aside. Amna stepped forward and pulled the bright pink fabric around my body. She pulled, stretched, and finally set it into place.

"Sundara!" She pressed her fingertips together and bowed slightly. Right about that time, the flap to the entrance opened. Raksha peeked in then smiled.

"Oh Abby, you look stunning!"

"What does sundara mean? What do I have on, Raksha? May I see it?" I asked her as I moved toward the exit. She nodded.

"It means beautiful, Abby. And not yet. Here, allow me to place this over you." Raksha held up a sheer fabric trimmed in a beautiful gold pattern that matched the bright pink I was wearing. She laid it across my shoulder then stepped back. She nodded and smiled. "Now we must decorate!"

I swallowed. "Decorate?"

She giggled and pulled me toward a table and sat me down. A few of the other women were pulling out jewelry that looked similar to what Raksha was wearing.

After make-up and jewelry had been applied, I was finally allowed to see the finished product of a culture I had no knowledge of. The mirror was turned toward me. In the reflection stood a woman I did not recognize. She had my face, but the make-up was not mine, the Bindi stone, as Raksha called it, had been placed in the center of my forehead. It led to the beautiful crown on my head.

My hair was parted down the middle and the stones of the crown lay across it. The sides of it came down toward my ears. Then there was the necklace I had on. It had a beautiful pink stone in the center of it and the gold chain was cool against my skin.

"Raksha, I... wow... I don't know what to say."

"Give thanks to Bhau-beej," she told me. "This is the day to celebrate the bond between brothers and sisters." She bowed slightly with a smile. "Today, you may be my sister and be part of my family."

I wasn't sure how to take this, or accept it. I had not been instantly invited into someone's family like this before. I wasn't sure how to feel about this... gratitude, yes. But there was something else, something stronger than just gratitude. There was hope. This made me smile and my eyes blurred slightly from the threat of tears.

Raksha then hugged me and I felt her nod.

I hugged her back and smiled.

"Okay, show me around!" I asked as I inhaled to control the emotions I was feeling.

I'm not sure how much time had passed, but the sun had begun its descent. Raksha pulled me back toward her hut and we sat in a few fold out chairs. I was excited to experience this new culture, but I was also exhausted. Walking around, smiling, and talking to people, then tasting all the amazing food… it was exhausting… and so much fun!

The fireworks started and it was followed by oohs and ahhs from the people watching. I glanced to those around me and enjoyed their smiles.

"When do you go back to America, Abby?" Raksha asked me.

"I'm not sure, yet," I told her. "I am supposed to go to Australia next, but I may venture back to Scotland first." I smiled and lowered my gaze. I also felt my face blush as I thought of Clive.

"Oh, is there someone in Scotland who waits for you?"

I nodded. "Something like that."

"And what of your family back home? Have they met this man?"

I shook my head. "They have not and I doubt they ever will." This was a subject I did not wish to discuss at a celebration like this.

Then again, I wanted to discuss this in the Ashram, but I could never get anyone there to take the time. Maybe this was a sign?

"Why is that?" She asked me. "Please, I do not wish to pry, but I cannot understand how parents do not support their children."

"How much do you know about American culture?" I asked her.

"Not much, it seems." She crossed her legs toward me and adjusted herself in her seat. "If you would like to discuss, I would like to listen."

I nodded and lowered my gaze. Raksha took me into her home, dressed, and decorated me, as she stated. Now she wanted to know about my family. I sighed.

"My family dynamics are not the norm, Raksha."

"Norm? What is norm?"

"Oh, normal. I'm sorry. My family is not what would be considered normal."

"Okay," she paused and allowed me to continue.

I opened up and told her about my father and his business, my mother and her drinking, the verbal abuse, the fact my father had been having an affair and my going to Scotland to "find myself."

She nodded and listened contently. She only asked questions when they were needed, like, "why would he leave you with her?" and "why would she ever say such dreadful things?"

My answer to both was, "I don't know."

Raksha took my hand and squeezed it. "May God be with you, Abby. You are a lovely person. You do not deserve what you have been dealt. No one deserves that. So trust me when I say good fortune will be yours."

"What do you mean?" I asked her. I couldn't believe how good it felt to talk to Raksha, to tell her how I was feeling. She squeezed my hand once more.

"You seek to find closure on your past and understand what your future might be. Don't allow the negative to dictate your positive, Abby. If you find your path, follow it, even if that path leads you to Scotland." She winked then released my hand.

I smiled and averted my gaze. "I have been spending time in the Ashram, but unfortunately, I haven't been able to have someone talk to me while I've been there." I looked back to her. "You have given me that tonight. Thank you very much." I willed myself not to cry. When I felt a tear threaten to escape, I reached up and wiped my eye to prevent it.

"God sometimes places people in our paths for a reason. Tonight, we were each other's."

I nodded, then leaned over and hugged her tightly. "Thank you so much."

"You are quite welcome, Abby of America." She giggled and

pulled back, then she winked. "Enjoy the festivities. The sari is yours."

"Sorry?" I asked her.

She shook her head. "Sari, the outfit clothing you. It is yours."

"What? No, I can't accept this!" I touched the dress, the head-piece I had on.

"Yes, you can and you will. It is my gift to you on this day of Diwali." She stood and held her hand out to me. "Now if you would, join me as we celebrate in the street with a dance!

15

J made it back to my room a little sweaty from the dancing, and absolutely full from all the food I had eaten. I began removing my garments and thought of Clive. I missed his smile and his laugh. I think he would have encouraged the adventure today. I think he would have taken part in it. The man would have absolutely had a ball dancing around and not only been entertained, he would have also been the entertainer. Maybe, once my adventures were over, I'd bring him back here for Diwali.

I took a shower and cleaned up. My new jewelry sat on my bathroom sink and I touched it lightly. The pink stone was beautiful. I pulled on a satin nightgown then ventured toward my laptop. Thinking of Clive, I pulled up my email and found a message from him. I opened it and in it was a picture of him... in the bathroom... naked. I grinned and followed that up with a laugh. Clive was posing in the image like he was pointing to something, with both arms. He reminded me of a male model.

Suddenly, my Skype rang. "Speak of the devil." I clicked on accept and video chat. Clive's image filled my screen and I smiled. "Well, hello there, handsome devil. Nice picture."

"Hey, beautiful, looking good. How've ye been? Miss me yet?" He chuckled. "Stand up and spin for me. Let me see ye beauty."

I thought it would be fun to pose for Clive so I stood and moved across my room. I kept myself in view of the camera as I stepped back. "Would you like me to do anything in particular?"

Clive's brows rose in surprise. He cleared his throat and the grin he wore lit up his face. "Aye, do me a strip tease, beautiful."

I felt my face begin to blush. I shook my head and let out a soft laugh. "Well, I need some music, so hang on." I came back to my laptop, bent over, and brought up Pandora.

"Aye, baby, keep like that. I can see down ye shirt." Clive chuckled. I shook my head then the music started.

I stepped back across the room and kept my back to the camera. Slowly, to the sounds of Audioslave, I began to lift my nightgown over my head. My long hair tumbled down my back and I looked over my shoulder at the camera. Clive was smiling and sitting back in his chair.

Keeping my back to the camera, I slowly pushed my panties down my hips. I bent over, purposely exposing my ass and legs to the camera.

"Oh hell, woman, ye are killing me!"

I grinned and kicked my panties away.

"Ye are making me hard!"

I snorted at this then covered my lips with my fingers. I turned to face the camera. "Do you like what you see?" I took my hands and slowly ran them down my breasts to my abs.

"Aye, woman! Shit, do me a favor and touch yerself."

"Oh my gawd, Clive!" I laughed and shook my head. "Only if you do it for me, too."

"Aye, baby, I can definitely do that."

Suddenly, Clive stood and he disappeared. I waited for a moment and when he returned, he was not only naked; he was hard. The man was not lying. I pursed my lips together to keep from giggling.

Never had I done anything like this with anyone. I took in a deep breath then slowly exhaled. Clive licked his lips and by the movement of his arm, I could tell he was stroking himself. He continued watching me.

"Woman, if ye were here, I would have ye on ma bed, having ma way with ye. I would pin ye down and tie yer sweet lil ass to ma bed. Fuck me, woman!"

"Sounds interesting, Clive. I've never been tied up or forced down." I slowly reached between my legs and gasped softly. "What else would you do?"

He told me a few other positions he would put me in and only under his command, would he allow me to release. I have never been in a dominant relationship before, but he honestly had me intrigued.

This back and forth went on for a while before Clive finally climaxed. He relaxed in his chair and watched me. He made a motion with his hand to continue. I blinked.

"You… you want me to get off over Skype?" I felt the heat of embarrassment rush up my neck and cover my face and ears. I could do this in the bedroom, hell, I've DONE this in the bedroom. But like this? This was new territory for me.

"Baby, holy fuck!" he exclaimed. "I want to see ye touch yerself, woman. Show me how ye like it."

I swallowed and let out a breath I didn't realize I had been holding until now. I lowered my gaze to my thighs. Quickly, I glanced at my suitcase. I'd brought a toy with me, but did I tell him this? I grinned slyly then my gaze rose to the camera.

"Hold on." He nodded and I stood. I crossed the room to my suitcase. I opened one of the zipped pouches and pulled out my vibrator. I knew being on this trip alone, I would need… assistance. I bit my lip and stared at the pink device. The clit stimulator stared back at me, almost daring me to do it.

I sighed, made my way back to the camera, and sat down.

Slowly, I raised the vibrator to the camera. If Clive's face had not lit up earlier, it sure did now.

"Aye, oh baby! Now we're talking!" He clapped his hands once and rubbed them together. "Aye, this I will enjoy!" He chuckled and relaxed back in his chair.

"Clive," I started and lowered my gaze. "I've never done anything like this."

"Would ye do it if we were in the same room?"

I looked back at the camera. I nodded once.

"What is so different about now?"

"Umm, I don't know, I guess I'm just... shy?"

He chuckled. "Woman, ye are anything but shy. Now," he grinned once again, "touch yerself. Yer in a safe place, Abby. Trust me when I tell ye that ye have nothing to worry about." He winked. "Only one thing though."

"Hmm? What's that?" My throat suddenly felt dry.

"Ye cannot cum until I tell you to."

I blinked. "What? I can't stop myself if I'm going to cum."

He nodded once then leaned forward. "Aye, ye can. Ye will not do it until I tell ye to. Understood?"

I sighed and nodded. "Okay. I'll try."

He smiled. "That's ma girl. Now, fuck yerself."

Holy shit, what had I gotten myself into with Clive? I was actually more turned on at the prospect of performing in front of him, and also this dominant submissive game he was playing. Maybe it was not a game, but whatever this was, I was actually turned on. He was somewhat aggressive when we were together, but this... this was different. And I liked it.

I grasped the vibrator in my hand and bent my legs to rest my heels on the chair. I turned on the device and it began to buzz. Clive's grin widened only slightly. I closed my eyes and began to lower it when he spoke up.

"No, love, look at me."

I opened my eyes and stared into the camera. I touched myself and the vibrations caused me to gasp and jump. I did it again and this time, I relaxed into it.

"Good girl," he started. "How does it feel?"

"It's nice," I whispered.

"I can't hear ye. Did you say ye wished it were me?"

I grinned. "Yes, I wish it were you." My head lay back on the chair and my eyes closed.

"No, baby, lift yer head and look at me."

"Clive, don't, let me do this."

"WOMAN!" He yelled and instantly I raised my head in alarm. "I want ye to look at me when ye do this. Now, do not disobey me again. Understood?"

I nodded, glad to see he did not appear upset, aside from the tone of his voice.

"Have ye been in a dominant relationship before, Abby?"

I swallowed and moaned softly as the vibrations continued against my sex. "No," I shook my head. "I've never been much of a relationship kind of girl. Well, at least until now."

"Oh, is that so?" He asked, intrigued. He leaned forward and pointed down. "Lower the camera. Allow me to watch."

I did as he requested and reached for the camera. I lowered it and closed my eyes. I moaned softly and continued the ministrations.

"That's right, baby, keep going. Fuck, ye are making me hard again."

"I bet you would like me to take you in my mouth." My eyes opened sharply at my own words. Did I seriously just say those words?

Clive chuckled. "Fuck me, baby. Aye, I would."

I pushed the camera back up and I'll be damned if he watched me without looking at me. I understood, somewhat, the thrill of looking into the eyes of the one you wished to conquer. Normally, it is me, but now? Now it is Clive. I want him to dominate me. I need him to. I need...

"Oh my god, Clive...."

"Not yet, doll, not yet." He licked his lips and I removed the vibrator for a moment.

"If not, I need to stop so I don't."

He nodded. "Push yer fingers inside ye and let me see yer honey."

As he requested, I pushed a finger inside, then brought it to the camera. He grinned with an approving nod.

"Ye may finish, love."

"Oh yes!" I quickly pressed the vibrator against me again and turned it on high. I moaned louder and my body quivered, then bucked as I came. "Oh my GOD! Oh shit!"

When I finished, I set the toy down and worked to calm my heaving chest. As I glanced at the camera, Clive licked his lips. I grinned.

"What is it?" I asked.

"I'm flying there tomorrow. I'm coming just to fuck ye."

I laughed and shook my head. "I'll be back soon enough, silly. Can you wait for me?" I thought about what I was asking. Does he want me to come back? Does he expect me to? What about Texas? It is not as if anything is waiting for me there.

"That's true, I guess, but dammit woman, I want ye!" He growled.

"Clive, when my trip to Australia is over, do you want me to come back to Scotland?" I blinked and lowered my gaze. I didn't want to see the look on his face. I did not want him to see the disappointment if he said no, or even maybe.

"Are ye kidding me, love? Aye, hell, ye better come back here!"

I quickly looked back at the camera and smiled. "Really?" Hell, I sounded like an excited school girl, but I didn't care.

"Aye, woman! If I were not so tied up with the bar and the distillery, I would come to India, or Australia, and bring ye back with me."

I smiled at this. I felt something inside me begin to change. I'm not sure if it was due to the meditation in the Ashram, my time with Clive, or maybe the time alone with myself, or if it was a mix of all of the above. Whatever it was, I loved how I felt and nothing, absolutely nothing could change that.

"All right, woman. Well, it is late. I need to shower and head on to bed. You need to sleep as well. Thank you for an amazing evening of sex... without sex." Clive gave me a lopsided grin. "What time is it there?"

We talked for a few more minutes, exchanged our good nights, and then ended our conversation. I closed my laptop and sat back with a smile. I glanced down at myself and laughed.

"I just had internet sex with Clive." I shook my head then rose to head toward my bathroom to clean up.

The next morning, I stretched and yawned in my bed. I felt alive, felt aware of myself, and my surroundings. I had not felt like this in quite some time, if ever. I would be leaving for Australia in a few days and then back to Scotland. I needed to discuss this with my parents. I didn't think my father would care too much but my mother would care even less, sad to say. I sighed, not wanting to think about her.

I climbed out of bed and got myself ready for the day. Pulling on a black t-shirt with the words, *Johnny Cash, Man in Black* written across the front, I paired it with a pair of denim jeans and wedge sandals. My hair was pulled to the side and braided. I pushed my sunglasses onto my face then headed outside.

The hotel called a taxi for me. He asked where I would like to go. "Shopping?" The cabbie nodded and took off from the hotel. Half an hour drive later, he pulled up to a mall that was bigger than anything I could have expected.

Bloomingdales, H&M and many other stores were here for the taking. I smiled and almost felt like I was home. My smile faltered slightly as I thought about the Indian family from last night. Maybe I could bring them here with me and take them shopping.

I smiled to this thought and nodded to myself. Maybe I could find something for Raksha.

I stepped inside the mall and as soon as the cool, air conditioned air hit me, and the familiar smell of new clothes, I felt at ease. Shopping was therapy for me; my mother taught me this.

If anyone pisses you off, go charge up their credit card.

Well, this was my credit card I would charge up. Not that I couldn't pay it off immediately, but still... I sighed and found myself in the women's department.

As I was reaching for a cute pair of slacks, my phone rang. I pulled out my phone and recognized the area code as Dallas. I rolled my eyes and shoved it back into my bag. I pulled the pants off the rack then found a cute, light yellow top. My phone rang again. I sighed and pulled it out once more. This time it was my father's office.

"Why is Daddy trying to reach me?" I sighed and pressed ANSWER. "Yes, Daddy?"

"Abby Masters?"

The voice was not my father's. This was not unusual. His officers occasionally phoned me.

"Yes? This is Abby."

"Miss Masters, this is Deputy Lang. Your father has been in an accident. We were told you were overseas."

I felt a little numb. Is it normal to call the children when their father has been in an accident? Well, family members yes, but his office? "Oh no," I was silent for a moment, then continued. "Is he okay? I mean, since you're calling, you're telling me he's okay, right?" I knew I was rambling and I also knew, deep down, if he was okay, no one would have called. I might have received a letter or email about it.

"No, Miss Masters. It would be best if you returned home as soon as possible. He's in critical condition and... if I may be honest, it doesn't look good."

I froze. I held my breath. I dropped the clothes I was holding and stood there. Next was my phone. My mouth was slack jawed and I just stared at the wall across from me.

"Allo?" A sales associate with beautiful, long black hair approached me with a smile. "Umm... madam?" She spoke English and I turned to face her.

"I'm sorry, I need to go." I bent over and picked up my phone. "Deputy, please have my father's secretary make arrangements for me to return home on an emergency flight."

He cleared his throat. "Miss Masters... his secretary was with him when it happened. She did not make it."

"Oh hell," I closed my eyes and inhaled deeply, then slowly released it. "Has anyone contacted my mother yet?" I did not want to be the one to do it. Who knows how she would take it. If it were anyone else, she would make a big show about it.

"Yes, ma'am. Word has been issued to her."

"How was she?" I asked. I felt remarkably... calm. I knew if she was hysterical, they would look to me for answers. If my mother was calm, she would most likely tell everyone to go to hell and that he'd gotten what he deserved. I can hear her now in my head.

"Honestly, ma'am, I don't know. Should I have someone here take care of the arrangements for you?"

"No, no, that's okay. I can take care of it. His secretary would usually take care of this for us," *among other things*, I thought to myself.

"All right. I'll send word that you are returning. Please let us know your scheduled flight time and we'll have a car there to pick you up."

$\sim$

I made it back to my hotel and called our travel agent. Maggie answered and the familiar sound of her voice, the southern accent... it had a small effect on me. I'm not sure why, but most likely, the shock of what has happened is wearing off.

I explained why I was returning and that I needed a ticket to come home ASAP. Maggie offered her sympathy then found me a ticket back to Dallas that would arrive the following afternoon. Maggie was a goddess. I thanked her and hung up the phone. I stared at my laptop for a moment. I needed to tell Clive, or at least let him know.

Drafting an email to him, I stared at it, having no idea how to word that I was going back to Texas and I would be in touch.

Dear Clive,

My father has been in an accident in Texas. I'm headed back tonight and should be there tomorrow afternoon. My trip to Australia is on hold, obviously. I'll be in touch to let you know what happens and when I can return to Scotland. You have my number. Please call me so I can hear your voice.

Love, Abby

I pressed send, then closed my laptop and packed. Within the hour, I was at the airport, through security, and on my plane. My eyes burned from the threat of tears, exhaustion, and the fact I was headed back to the place I'd purposely left.

The deep, sinking feeling I'd felt earlier while talking to Maggie had returned with a vengeance. I swallowed hard and felt like I was going to retch. I did not want to go home. I wanted to stay as far away as I could, but I had to go back. This was my father.

I needed a *Xanax*, immediately.

About 18 hours and one connecting flight later, I landed in Dallas. My stomach was in knots. I took my time leaving the plane. First class was first to get off, but honestly, I wanted to be in the back of the plane. I did not want to be here. It's not that I was being selfish; I simply did not want to face my mother or my past. I'd had a chance to start over and it was liberating. Now I felt like I had walked back into the hell that I had freed myself from.

I made my way toward the terminal and found a driver holding up my name on a banner.

"I'm Abby Masters. I need my bag off the belt." The driver, a middle-aged man who stood about six feet tall, with a medium build and tan, nodded. I described what it looked like then pointed at it once I saw it coming. He grabbed the bag then we made our way to the waiting limo. He opened the door for me and I slipped inside.

The seats were chilly from the air blowing in the car. I sighed and tried to relax, but couldn't. I fished my cell from my purse and turned it on. Soon, a few messages and emails came across as alerts. I pulled the emails up and smiled when I saw something from Clive.

Dearest Abby,
My thoughts will be with you. Let me know what happens. I'll be there when you need me, not if.
Love, Clive

I smiled at the message and as I was about to reply, the driver's door opened and the car illuminated.

"We're ready, Miss Masters. I'm to take you directly to the hospital."

I nodded and put my phone away. And with it, the thought of messaging Clive back. "Have you seen or heard from my mother?"

He shook his head. "No, ma'am, but I'm sure she has her phone with her if you would like to call."

"Thank you, but I'll wait till we arrive."

We rode in silence until Baylor All Saints Hospital came into view. I glanced up to the large, bright letters on the hospital building and swallowed hard.

I hated hospitals. Hated them. Blaine had been admitted a few years back for overdosing. My mother had been admitted for depression and suicide attempts. She'd also been admitted before for alcohol abuse. I hated being here.

The driver opened my door and the warm, humid air of Texas blew inside. I did not want to escape the car. I wanted to remain inside where it was safe. He cleared his throat and glanced down at me.

I felt my heart pick up rhythm. I felt my stomach turn. I pursed my lips and turned in the seat. My feet touched the concrete and as I stood, flashes from photographers went off in my face.

My hands covered my eyes and the driver wrapped his arms around me and held me close. "I'm sorry, Miss Masters. I did not realize the reporters would be here."

"Just... just get me inside!"

Rushing through the crowd, I was escorted into the hospital. The media was not allowed to follow us past the doors and for once, I was grateful for being on the inside. I wanted to turn and run, but they would only follow.

"Thank you," I whispered.

He nodded. "I'll wait down here until you are ready to leave. I'll be out in the car." He handed me a business card. "This is to the phone in the car. Call me when you're ready."

I took it and slipped it into my pocket. "Thank you." Facing the information desk, I told her my father's name. Her eyes opened wide, then she busied herself and dropped a pen.

"Y-Yes, he's up in room 1243, Miss Masters. Shall I escort you?"

I shook my head. "Not necessary." A moment later, the elevator opened and two men in black suits appeared. "The cavalry is here." The nurse smiled and nodded a few times.

In the past, I used to eat this attention up. I could never get enough of it. Now? Hell, I just want to blend into the wall and become a big fat nothing. I did not want to be here. I wanted my father to be okay, but not here.

My escorts stood on either side. I glanced up to them. "Is he okay?" I asked, but neither of them answered. Great.

The doors opened and the guard on my right stepped out first. "This way, ma'am." The other guard followed close behind me. The nurses at their stations looked up. I heard whispers of "poor little girl," "look, there's the man's daughter," and "her mother is in hysterics."

Great, just what I wanted to hear.

The guard opened the door to the room and it was dark. I heard beeps from a machine. The room smelled like cleaning solution and... death. I closed my eyes and stepped farther into the room. The opening of the door must have let in a little light because my mother stepped into it.

She was crying, or had been crying. Her makeup was a mess. She sniffed and held out her arms to me. I stared at her for a moment. She was either drunk or putting on a show... probably both.

"Oh honey, you're finally here! Oh, come here!" She cried and pulled me close to her. She smelled of alcohol, vomit, and cigarettes. She lowered her voice so only I would hear her, "Well, look who finally decided to come home, you ungrateful little bitch."

I squeezed my eyes closed and told myself not to cry. I shook my head. "Whatever you say, Mother. Let me see Daddy." I pulled myself away and sidestepped around her. When my eyes went to the bed, I gasped. I didn't recognize him. He was bandaged, had a black eye, tubes in his mouth and nose and a machine was next to him. I recognized it immediately. He wasn't breathing on his own.

A tear quickly betrayed me and slid down my cheek. I wiped it away and stepped closer. I bent over the bed and my lower lip began to tremble. I kissed his forehead.

"Daddy," I whispered, "I'm here. I'm here, Daddy."

The door opened again and this time, a few nurses walked inside. I stood and wiped my tears, then turned my gaze to them.

My mother stood behind them, arms crossed over her body and she pinched the bridge of her nose.

"What is going on?" I asked in a soft voice.

"We have orders, Miss Masters. We are here to turn off the respirator per your father's request."

"WHAT?" The glare at my mother did not go unnoticed. She gave it back to me, and a smirk.

"Per your father's request, Miss Masters," the other nurse chimed in, "he had a DNR statement filled out in his will. We kept him alive long enough for you to arrive."

Somewhere in the conversation, I tuned them out. I went numb. I felt nothing, saw nothing, heard nothing. Someone touched my shoulders and I felt myself being shook. I was then escorted out of the room into the waiting area.

"Do you have someone we can call?" one of the nurses asked me, "or should we leave you with your mother?"

This brought me from my daze. "No. Here," I leaned over and pulled out the card the driver gave me. "Call this number. Tell him I'll be down shortly."

he funeral was a few days later. We had the viewing shortly after his death. His secretary had already been buried by her family. I sat in my room in our house and stared at myself in the mirror. I had on a black knee length dress that was sleeveless, lace around the collar and bottom of the hem. I wore black pumps on my feet. My hair was pulled to the side in a braid. My make-up was set and I could only sit still.

A light tap on my door grabbed my attention.

"Go away," I announced.

"Abby?"

I knew that voice. I turned toward the door and blinked. "Lexi?" The door opened and sure enough, Lexi and Makayla both stood in the doorway. I bit the inside of my lip to keep from crying. I put Lexi through hell with Blaine and Bobby Ray, yet here she was.

Lexi immediately crossed the room and pulled me into her arms, Makayla right behind her. The three of us hugged for a few minutes and I began to lose my resolve.

"He's dead. My father is dead," was all I could manage.

Neither of the girls said anything. We stood holding onto one another. After a few minutes, Lexi pulled away first. She smiled and wiped her fingers under my eyes.

"We'll be here as long as you need us to be, okay?"

I nodded and lowered my gaze. "I am so sorry, for everything."

"No, don't do that, not now, okay?" Lexi demanded. "It has been a long time since all that shit happened. We're here for you, okay?"

I nodded then made my way back to my vanity. "My mother hates me," I announced. "She is trying to blame me for this accident. Did you know that?"

Makayla sat down on her knees in front of me. She took my hands in hers and pulled my attention to her. "Come stay with me. You don't need to be here."

"The will reading is later. I have to be here for that," I told them.

"We can be here with you, if you want?" Makayla told me.

I nodded. "Please?"

"You don't even have to ask," Lexi told me. "I am curious, though. You were in Scotland, right?"

"Well, yes, but in India when the call came in," I told her.

"Right. Help me understand how your father's accident was your fault?"

I sighed and pulled my hands from Makayla's. I turned in my seat and looked to my reflection. "She thinks I drove my father away to his secretary. She thinks that everything that has ever happened is all my fault. From her drinking, to her acts of violence; everything is my fault." I pulled out my concealer and reapplied it.

"Did you know she tried to fuck one of the men at the modeling agency?" I turned to face the girls in my room. "She actually went up there, drunk, and told them she had a better body than I did and she wanted to show them. She then straddled one of the male agents and grinded her body against his." I shook my head. "They told us both to get the fuck out. Later, she told my father that I tried to fuck one of the agents and that's why I was thrown out. She told him I had to take the walk of shame out of there."

"Oh Abby, I had no idea," Lexi stated.

"Yeah, well there's a reason I never said anything. I was too embarrassed."

"I'm so sorry," Makayla said.

I nodded and re-applied my eye shadows, liner, and then mascara. "She even blames me for the affair my father had for years with his secretary."

"Seriously?" Makayla asked. I nodded.

"She welcomed me back to Texas by calling me an ungrateful bitch."

I glanced to Lexi and found her and Makayla looking to one another. "What is it?" I asked.

Lexi shook her head. "Nothing, just… well, this explains a lot is all."

"Explains, what, exactly?" I asked as I turned to face them.

"Everything," Makayla stated. "You know I went into psychology, right?" I nodded and she continued. "You long for something you cannot have. Whether it is the love of your mother and father, or the love of a man, you are constantly seeking something you can control." Both girls stared at me. "Am I right?"

I lowered my head and nodded. "I sort of figured that out about myself while I was gone."

"You did?" Makayla asked. "How?"

"I sort of met someone." I smiled and glanced up. "His name is Clive and he's in Scotland."

"Oh, does he wear a kilt?" Makayla asked.

I blinked. "Seriously?"

She looked down. "I'm sorry, that sort of just came out."

I fought it hard, but the smile broke through anyway. I giggled softly and both girls looked up at me. "Yes, he wears a kilt… traditionally!"

"OH MY GAWD!" Lexi yelled then laughed.

I filled them in on who Clive was, how we met, and our adventures together. I realized, once I was done, that I felt better and the thought of my father dying had been temporarily blocked from my mind.

Suddenly, my mother was at my bedroom door. "Well, I see a party is in order in the wake of your father's passing." She huffed and left the room.

"Ignore her," Lexi said.

I nodded a few times then stood. Letting out a long sigh, hating that my mother saw me with a semblance of happiness, "Well, shall we?" Both girls stood and each took my hands. "Oh, Lexi, where is your husband?" I had not seen Bobby Ray since he had been elected Senator of Texas, other than on the television.

"He sends his love, but could not be here. He's in DC right now."

I nodded and we made our way toward the bedroom door. "Please, don't let me fall." My voice came out in a whisper and I swallowed hard.

"We're right here beside you," Makayla said. "I promise; we won't let you fall or crumble. Okay?"

I nodded and we headed outside to where the car was waiting, with my mother inside it.

$\sim$

My y mother sat in the front row of the pew at our church, Makayla sat next to her, then me, then Lexi. I was grateful for the barrier, but felt bad for Makayla.

"Thank you," I whispered. She winked at me. The preacher came to the front of the pulpit and began. The funeral was for family and close friends only. The burial, however, would be open to anyone who could squeeze in. I was not looking forward to this.

The preacher finished his prayer, then turned to my mother and asked for her eulogy. She sure delivered. The woman went up and cried behind the pulpit. Everything she claimed about being a loving wife and mother, how he was there for his family and loved us unconditionally… damn, give the woman an academy award.

I squeezed Lexi's hand hard. She squeezed back, letting me know she was still there. When my mother finished her speech, she took a seat and glared at me in the process. The preacher then asked if I had a few words to share. I shook my head. I couldn't do it; I couldn't go up there and give a speech about a man I barely knew. I wouldn't do that to him or myself.

The preacher nodded and I assumed he thought I was too upset. In a way, I was. Next, my father's brother went up to the pulpit and gave a speech. At some point, I tuned everything out. I closed my eyes and recalled what I learned in the Ashram.

I inhaled deeply then slowly, let it go. I focused on my toes and settled them, then worked the feeling up my body. I thought of my father, the times we had together that were fun… like Christmas.

"Look to see what Santa brought you, baby!" The man smiled ear to ear. I unwrapped my gift with a quickness only an eight year old could.

"DADDY! IT'S A SUZY COOKS A LOT!" I grinned and held onto the small, pink oven with so much love. He took a few pictures of me. My mother looked on with a smile… that eventually shifted to a scowl.

Even before he cheated, before her drinking started, she hated how my father was with me.

Jealousy. She hated he was attentive to me and not her. She told me this daily.

"I wish you were never fucking born! You are a burden to me and your father!" I will never, ever forget these words and how she made me feel.

I felt a tap on my shoulder. I glanced sideways to Lexi.

"It's over. Are you ready to head outside?"

"What?" I glanced to the pulpit and the preacher was leaving the stand. I missed everything from my uncle and most likely, anything foolish my mother did. "It's over?" Lexi nodded.

"Are you okay?" She leaned in, "Did you fall asleep?"

I smiled and shook my head. "No, I didn't fall asleep. I learned meditation. I'm surprised how well it worked."

It took about twenty minutes for everyone to get into their cars and arrive at the gravesite. I stared out the window and watched as people lined up around the green tent. My mother exited the car first.

"Get out, girls. They won't wait for us." She closed the door and leaned against it. The driver took her arm and escorted her over to the grave. She put on the dramatics as she walked to the gravesite.

"They will wait for you, honey," Lexi told me. "Take all the time you need."

"No, I need to do this. I need to get this over and get the will reading done, then leave this god-forsaken state! I cannot do this with her, I can't. She hates me and trust me when I say it, the feeling is fucking mutual." I inhaled sharply then opened the door. "Let's go."

The outdoor funeral started. Amazing Grace, followed by Tim McGraw's "Live Like You Were Dying," played. The songs brought tears to my eyes. I wanted to cry for my father, for the man I barely knew. I wanted to cry for the daughter he left behind. I wanted to cry for the wife who left him so long ago. I needed to cry for me... but I couldn't.

I stared at the closed coffin. Slowly, it began to descend into the ground. I stood and approached it slowly and gazed downward. "Daddy," I whispered and fell to my knees. I heard a gasp and Lexi and Makayla were by my sides immediately. I broke down and sobbed.

"He's gone! He's gone! Oh my GOD, he's gone and I can't tell him I love him! I can't... he... oh my god, he's gone!" I sobbed and

Lexi pulled me close to her. She held me tight and Makayla had my backside.

I heard my mother mumble something about being ungrateful then she took a seat. My heart was broken. My father was gone. For all intents and purposes, my family was gone. My mother made it clear I was dead to her. What do I do now?

I pulled away from Lexi and looked at her. She wiped my tears and offered an encouraging smile.

"I love you," she whispered.

"Why?" I asked her. "I shit on you in a way no friend ever should."

She shook her head. "Stop it. It's behind us and frankly, I missed having you around." She hugged me again and I hiccupped.

When my knees began to hurt, I released her. "I need to stand. I need air. I need away from her," I whispered. I glanced at my mother and she glared back at me. I closed my eyes and lowered my head.

We stood and I dusted off my knees. When I looked up at the crowd, I froze. In the back was a man I never expected to see. I tried to smile but instead and almost immediately, my resolve faltered. My bottom lip trembled as he made his way toward me... kilt and all.

Clive pulled me close and held me as I cried into his chest. He kissed the top of my head and whispered softly to me. "Ahh now darling, shhh, it's okay, it's okay."

I felt another set of hands touch my back gently. "You must be Clive." I felt him nod. "I'm Lexi, childhood friend of Abby's. This is my cousin, Makayla."

"Nice to meet ye," he told them. "Cousins? Ye don't look anything alike."

"Cousins by marriage," Makayla told him.

"Ahh, I see. All right then, how about ye join me and Abby back at the hotel?"

I pulled back and looked up to Clive. "I have the reading of the will soon."

He nodded. "I shall go with ye then and wait outside. Once yer done, we shall head out." I watched him glance at who I could only assume was my mother. He sighed. "Guess it is time to meet the missus."

"No, you don't have to," I announced. I took his hand then reached for Lexi with the other. I glanced at Makayla and she nodded. "Where did you park, Clive?" He pointed to the direction of the car and the four of us left the burial site. I glanced once more toward my mother. If looks could kill, I think each of us would have died right then. I could only imagine what was running through her mind. Here shortly, I would find out, whether I wanted to or not.

a few days had passed since my father's funeral. We arrived at the attorney's office. Once inside, I took a deep breath and turned to face my army: Clive, Lexi, and Makayla. I nodded and released his hands, then left Clive in the hands of Lexi and Makayla. He kissed me softly and I turned toward the room. I glanced back at him once more before I stepped inside. As I shut the door behind me, the family attorney sat across from my mother at a polished oak desk that was big enough to hold fifteen people. I took a seat on the other side of the attorney. I wasn't ready for this. I think a part of me was still on auto-pilot. Maybe I was in shock.

My father was dead. My mother told me many times over she wished I was never born. Does this make me an orphan? Technically, no, but I might as well be. I sighed and cleared my throat. I crossed my legs and placed my hands in my lap.

Our family attorney had been with us for a good twenty years. The man was older, most likely in his seventies. He had a little hair left on his head and wore it slicked back. He smelled of Old Spice cologne. He wore a big gold ring on his finger that looked like a gold nugget.

He cleared his throat then opened the manila envelope. He took a quick read through the will before he began. He glanced at me, then at my mother, and then back down.

I felt nervous and my palms began to sweat. I glanced up at my mother to find her staring at the attorney like he was a huge steak and she had not eaten in months.

Honestly, it was disgusting.

"According to the will in place," he began. He glanced at me so quickly then adjusted himself in his seat. "All assets are hereby left to Abby Masters."

It suddenly felt like all the air in the room had been sucked out and I couldn't breathe. I stared at the table and my fists clenched in my lap.

"What?" My mother yelled. I felt the table move when she stood, but I did not dare look at her. "Are you fucking kidding me? He left everything to that... that bitch daughter of his?"

I closed my eyes and felt my eyes burn with tears. I felt my heart break in my chest. My head lowered slightly. He left me everything. Why? I inhaled a sharp breath and felt the pain of it when the air filled my chest.

"Mrs. Masters, the will clearly states right here..." he started before my mother cut him off.

"I DON'T GIVE A FUCK WHAT HIS FUCKING WILL SAYS! I WAS HIS WIFE! DAMMIT, ALL OF HIS IS MINE!" She slammed her fist on the table and the sound caused me to flinch.

"Mrs. Masters, you signed away your rights to it right here." The attorney held out a piece of paper that my mother snatched. I dared to glance in her direction and found her reading it with widened eyes. Her head shook back and forth and her mouth was agape.

"I do NOT remember signing this! This is BULLSHIT!" She seethed for a moment then made eye contact with me. Fear escalated inside my body and adrenaline spiked. "Where the fuck does this leave me?"

The attorney pushed away from the table and came to my side. "Well, to be honest, Mrs. Masters, a widow without a penny to your name. Your daughter now controls all assets, money, and any stocks and bonds your husband had. This includes the house you both live in."

"I don't want it," I mumbled.

"What's that?" The attorney said. My mother groaned and turned her back to us and walked across the room. She grabbed a hold of a desk and leaned against it.

"I don't want the house," I told him. "There's nothing there for me but bad memories. She can have it." My mother peeked at me over her shoulder, watching… calculating… like a lion watches its prey.

"Ms. Masters, if you so wish to sell the house, you may, that is your prerogative, but as for saying you do not want it, something must happen to it."

He placed his hand on my shoulder. "I'll set up a time with you to go over all the assets and see what we have in place. Will that be okay?" I looked up to him and nodded. "For what it's worth," he offered a hint of a smile, "I'm sorry for his abrupt passing. I understand the police are investing the death."

"Investigating for what? Is there something I do not know?" I asked.

He sighed and took a seat next to me. "He was shot in his car, as well as his secretary. There is suspicion of homicide."

I stared at him, long and hard, before I said anything. How did I miss this piece of information? Obviously my mother would not tell me. Why would she? Who would purposely want to kill my father? Who would wait until they knew he would be with his secretary? Who would shoot both of them? Who would…

I glanced across the room to my mother. A heated rage began to peak. I slowly rose from my chair and stared at her. She hated his secretary. She hated that he'd had an affair. She hated everything about her life, including me.

"Oh my god," I whispered. My hands began to shake and I fisted them. My nails dug hard into my palms. The attorney glanced between my mother and me. "Oh my god," I whispered again.

"What, you think *I* had something to do with this?" She turned to face me and crossed her arms over her chest. "That's ridiculous."

"Is it?" I asked. "You *hated* her, and as far as I can tell, you hated him as well."

She waved me off with a flip of her hand. "Just because I hated him doesn't mean I would kill him. Seriously, Abby? You really think I'm capable of such heinous things?"

I cocked a single brow and I gritted my teeth. No longer were my hands shaking, now it was my entire body. She had done it; I knew she had. She hated him and hated being married to him. She hated me. She hated everything about her life. I closed my eyes and tried to calm myself, but was failing… miserably.

A pair of hands rested on my arms from behind. A presence grazed against my back and a warm breath touched my ear. "Abby," Clive started, "Let's go. Not here, love. Not here."

"Let me go," I whispered. I had not realized he entered the room.

"No."

I opened my eyes and turned to face him. He had a sadness about him. He kept his hands on my arms and moved them up and down, slowly. "Abby, come on, let me take ye out of here." He leaned in slowly and rested his forehead on mine. In a whisper only I could hear, "The police are outside. We need to go."

"Where did you find him, Abby? Did you lie to him, too? Did you tell him that none of this is your fault? That you are a daddy's girl? Oh, did you tell him you fucked your best friend's man? How about all of Fort Worth and Dallas?"

I watched Clive as he glanced over my head at my mother. He

shook his head no and for a brief moment, his skin turned red. He exhaled then looked down to me. "Let's go, now."

I sighed and finally nodded.

"I'll be in touch," the attorney told me. I, again, nodded. He passed us and left the room. I didn't blame him for wanting to leave. I heard the faint sounds of walkie-talkies. The police were outside. Were they going to arrest my mother? Were they going to question me?

Clive took a hold of my hand and led me toward the door. Just as we were about to cross through the threshold, a pain seared my arm. A firm yank pulled me back and suddenly, I faced my mother.

"This is not over, you ungrateful little bitch!"

I sighed and lowered my gaze. My father had just died, and I'm ungrateful.

"Now ye listen to me, Mrs. Masters," Clive started. "We have not had the chance to officially meet, and with how this is going down, I know for certain ye are not someone I want around me, or someone I want around my Abby. Aye, she told me about what she did to Lexi. She told me why she did it. She has told me many things about herself ye may have no idea about. Unfortunately, now ye never will. Shame on you, woman and shame on you for calling yerself a mother."

Clive's grip tightened slightly on my arm and he pulled me toward him. I glanced once more at my mother, finding a shocked expression on her face. Everything he said, it was all true. It was everything I always wanted to say, but couldn't. She was all I had left… technically, but now… she was dead to me. I felt it in my heart.

If this is letting go, it fucking sucks.

I turned into Clive's chest and squeezed my eyes closed. His arms embraced my body and I felt him squeeze me slightly. I willed myself not to cry. I was afraid if he had not been holding me, I would have fallen down. I don't know if I could will myself to stand afterwards, but at least now, I didn't have to worry about that. Clive had me... I glanced up at him and found him looking one way then the other.

"This way," Lexi motioned. He nodded and followed her out.

"You are NOT going anywhere, young lady! Just because you found someone to fuck you doesn't mean..."

I tuned her out. I'd had enough. I couldn't do this with her, not anymore. I heard her as she continued her rant. She had been left with nothing. Clive's grip tightened and I heard him mumble something to me, but I'm not quite sure what it was.

We made it outside and the air was humid. The sun warmed my skin as we paused on the steps of the attorney's office. I closed my eyes and allowed the sun to warm my face.

Daddy, if you can hear me, I love you. I just wish you had told me... showed me you loved me, too.

"Get back here!" My mother had followed us outside. "What makes you think you can just walk out of here like you own the world? He may have left everything to you, but I will fight it! It is MINE! I spent my entire fucking marriage to a man who fucked someone else! Hell, if given the opportunity, he probably would have fucked you!"

Now I'd had enough. I heard Lexi and Makayla gasp. I heard what sounded like a growl come from Clive. I whirled on my mother, pulled my arm back, and punched her in the nose. She fell backward and screamed while she held her nose.

"GET THE FUCK AWAY FROM ME!" I panted heavily as the adrenaline pumped through my body. My fists clenched and released over and over. My teeth were gritted together and a pain shot through my jaw. I didn't care. I felt something and that was what was important. The moment I no longer felt anything, I knew I would be lost... I would then become my mother. "You don't love me. You never have! What do you want? The house? Fucking TAKE it! I don't want to go back there!

"Do you even know anything about Daddy? Do you know

WHY he fucked around on you? Let's consider some reasons, shall we?"

"Abby," Clive was behind me and touched my arms. "Love…"

"No," I looked at him over my shoulder, "I need to do this. It has been a LONG time in coming." He watched me for a moment then nodded.

I turned back to her and a sound erupted from my chest. I was snarling. I took a few steps toward her and she crawled back on the ground. "It was you. You drove him away! You and your damn jealousy! Your drinking! You… just you! You are awful, mean, and you hate everything and everyone! I am your daughter! You were supposed to protect me!" Tears ran down my cheeks as I continued. "You turned your back on me when I needed you most! You LEFT me!"

She looked to her left then her right. "I never left you, Abby. I'm right fucking here!"

"NO!" I screamed at her. I closed my eyes and took a deep breath, then slowly released it. "Did you ever consider how your actions would play on me or Daddy? Did you ever consider that? Or maybe telling me, day after day, that you wished I was never born? Or that I'd be no better than a whore who stripped for money? I AM YOUR DAUGHTER!" The last sentence came out as a scream. I was panting by the time I finished. My arms flailed to my sides for a moment, seeking some sort of purchase.

I found it by way of Clive's arms. He pulled me against him, my back to his chest. He held me tight, like a swaddle. His lips were close to my ear as he whispered to me, "It's okay, let it out. I'm here, yer friends are here." He paused for a moment as I felt myself begin to break down. "Let's go. Ye never have to see her again."

I heard a sniffle behind me. I turned to gaze at Lexi and Makayla, they were both crying. Lexi approached me first, tentatively, then held her arms out. My adrenaline was fading. My lip trembled and I rushed to her. She held me tight and rubbed my back.

"You stupid fucking bitch!" I heard my mother, but I made no move to do anything or answer her. I was done.

I felt a body behind me embrace our hug. It was Makayla. "We have you, honey. She will no longer hurt you. Let's go."

Clive's hand smoothed down my hair. "I'll pull the car around." I felt Lexi nod. She pulled me closer, tighter.

"Get over here, now!" She was moving closer. I could smell the stink of betrayal.

"NO!" Makayla released me and turned on her. "No, you are done! Do NOT make me hit you, Mrs. Masters, because I will! I have NO issue kicking your ass right now! And trust me when I say I can, I will!"

She gasped. "You wouldn't DARE!"

I heard Makayla laugh. "Care to test that theory?"

Lexi pulled away from me for a moment to intervene.

"No, let her. She deserves no less than a good ass whooping." I crossed my arms over my chest and glared at the woman I once called Mother.

A horn sounded behind us and when I turned, Clive stepped out of his rental car. "Let's go, Abby. Ye are done here, love."

My brow rose as I turned and glared at my mother. "My attorney will be in touch. I suggest packing what you have and find somewhere else to go."

"But you said you didn't want the house," she said with a little bit of a whine in her voice.

I rolled my eyes. "Doesn't mean I want YOU in it. Get your shit and be gone. You have thirty days." I turned my back on her and took the steps down to the road. Clive came around and opened the passenger door for me. I sat down inside and leaned against the seat. He closed the door then set off for the driver's seat.

"We'll meet you at the bar?" I heard Lexi ask.

"I'll have Abby call ye soon. Give her some time to recover then we will see."

I didn't hear anything else, other than the woman who was formally my mother sobbing on the attorney's steps. Because she was still my mother, technically, I wanted to go to her and hold her, tell her it would all will work out. I'm human after all. I'm not a sadist.

The other part of me, the rational part, wanted to turn away and never see her again. If she were to die, right now, would I miss her? Probably not. Like with my father, I will cry for the girl who never had her parents. I will cry for the girl who lost who she was in a matter of a week. I will cry because I do not know what else to do.

The police on sight ventured inside the house, my assumption was to interview my mother... no... not my mother.

I put my seat belt on as Clive put the car into drive. He took off and I watched the woman on the steps crying grow smaller and smaller the farther away we drove.

A few weeks had passed by since my father died. More details came out from his accident. The police sorted out the details and found he was shot while driving with his secretary. This part I knew already.

What I didn't know, upon further investigation, was the person who shot them was located. When I was questioned if I knew the man involved, I told them no. The police interrogated the man and found out that the woman who had formerly been my mother had hired him to kill my father and his secretary.

This was a shock to discover, obviously, but I think a part of me was not surprised. She hated him, I just didn't realize how much.

"She probably assumed everything would go to her," I told Clive. I crossed my legs in my chair. We were having dinner at the local Olive Garden in town.

"What is this soup, salad, and breadstick fuckery?" he asked.

I giggled. It felt good to smile. Everything was still so fresh and I felt almost guilty for smiling, for laughing. "You don't have to get all that, baby. Get whatever you like. My treat."

He glanced up to me with a smirk. "I want ye over this table. That's what I want."

I grinned and lowered my gaze. I felt a blush creep up my cheeks. "Well, maybe later."

"Definitely later, love. Definitely later."

I smiled and shook my head. "Anyway... I wonder when my father changed the will." I was talking more to myself than anything.

"Ye could ask yer attorney," he started, "or just let it go."

I nodded. Letting go was good. It seemed to be my mantra lately.

"I saw the reports on the telly about her being arrested. She did not take it well," he told me then shoved a piece of breadstick in his mouth.

I shrugged slightly. "Why would she? In her mind she probably thinks she did nothing wrong."

We finished our meal then headed back to the hotel we were sharing. I was not ready to go back into the house I grew up in. I had settled things with the family attorney... well, my attorney now... and put the house up for sale. I hired movers to pull my clothes out of my closet, wrote down the things I wanted and handed the keys over to the real estate agent. I provided my new forwarding address. I had set up a PO Box in town and given the information to Makayla and Lexi. They both agreed to check in on the box from time to time, and forward anything I needed to me.

Where would I go now? I wasn't sure, but eventually I would figure it out.

"I need to return to Scotland soon," Clive told me as the room door shut behind us.

I nodded. "I know." I crossed the room and stood in front of the sliding balcony door. Our suite was huge; it was like being in a large condo or apartment in the city.

Clive came up behind me and placed his hands on my shoulders. He kissed my neck softly. I tilted my head to the side slightly, offering him more of me. He slipped a hand to my cheek and turned my face toward him.

I looked into his beautiful green eyes. He smiled softly then looked at my lips. He leaned in and kissed me ever so gently. I turned into him and slipped my arms up, around his neck. His hands moved down to my waist and he pulled me close.

"How about a hot bath?" His lips were still kissing mine when he asked me this. I nodded.

"Only if you join me," I told him.

"Oh, I plan on it, love." He chuckled softly then deepened the kiss. His hands moved from my waist to my ass. He squeezed me, forcing me closer. My fingers moved into his hair and I tugged softly. "Keep that up, love, I'll fuck ye right now."

I grinned against his lips. "I remember something about fucking me long and hard… while I was in India?" I knew I was playing with fire… and I didn't care.

Clive growled and kissed me harder. He pushed against me until my back met the wall. He reached for my wrists then pressed my arms above my head. "I plan on doing just that, woman." He kissed me again and moved his lips to my jawline, then to my neck. He nibbled on my skin then my earlobe. I sighed as he pinned me against the wall.

"Bath tub or bed?" I questioned, gasping when his knee moved between my legs. He reached between my thighs and pressed his hand against my sex. His fingers teased against my clit and I moaned softly.

"Stop talking," he told me in a husky voice. I was going to lose myself in a moment. My panties were wet and I wanted them off, right now.

"Clive," I breathed his name. Suddenly, he stopped. He glared at me and his eyes narrowed.

"I said stop talking."

My brows rose in a questioning glance. My lips parted to say something and he shook his head no. He pulled away from me slightly, but left his fingers. He began his ministrations again. I closed my eyes with a soft moan.

"No, look at me, woman."

I opened my eyes once again and bit my lip. I gasped softly and pulled against the hold on my arms. He kept this up and I knew I would cum very soon.

His forehead touched mine and his fingers moved harder and faster. I moaned a little louder and my back arched.

"Mmm… I do so love pleasing ye, woman."

I offered a mischievous grin. "Release my arms, Clive. Now."

He shook his head no.

"Please? I wish to do something for you." I grinned softly then moaned as he continued teasing me.

"All right," he released my arms and removed his fingers. The initial invasion had been abrupt, but my body yearned for him to touch me again. I placed my palms on his chest and pushed him toward the bed. He sat down and stared up into my eyes.

I made a move to my knees and grabbed for his pants. "What are ye… Abby… Oh hell, woman!" He grinned and moved my hands away, then quickly removed his pants and boxers. Clive was very hard and absolutely ready for me. I kept his gaze and lowered my head. I licked his tip and he grinned. He reached for my hair and gathered it into his hands. As I took him into my mouth, he applied just a faint amount of pressure. I pulled back and he pushed me back down.

~

*I*t did not take Clive long to cum. We made it to the tub and relaxed. I leaned against his chest and his strong arms surrounded me. My back to his chest, I rested my head on his shoulder.

He kissed my forehead, my nose, my cheek, and my lips. I felt safe, secure, and felt like I belonged to him.

Which sent another question to mind: Did I return to Scotland with him? Did he want me to?

I swallowed hard and considered how to ask this question. I shifted myself against him, getting a more comfortable position. Clive must have felt my reluctance.

"Is everything all right, love?"

I didn't answer right away. I lifted away from him and moved to the other side of the tub. My back to the tub, I lifted my gaze to his. "Yes and no," was the best I could come up with, considering the coming conversation.

"All right," he furrowed his brows, "want to tell me what's on ye mind?"

"I…" I hesitated then tried again. "When you head back to Scotland, what… what will…"

"Are ye coming with me?" he asked, finishing my thought.

The water was hot and I knew my skin was already flushed, but I also knew my blood was rushing to my cheeks. I nodded softly.

"Ye better be, woman."

I immediately met his gaze. "What?"

"I don't plan on returning to Scotland without ye." He grinned. "I don't think there is much holding ye here, right?"

I nodded. "Right."

"Then come with me." He moved across the tub toward me. His eyes were dark and seductive. He immediately kissed me. It was soft, but wanting. He pushed my legs apart and settled between them. "I plan on making love to ye every fucking day, woman." He continued to kiss me. I felt his hardness rub against my thigh and I grinned.

I reached for him and gently wrapped my fingers around his erection. He moaned softly against my lips. He pulled me to the edge of my seat in the tub then positioned himself in front of me.

I felt him enter of me. His cock was warm from the water and when he filled me, I gasped. "I love the sounds ye make," he told me. "Fuck, ye turn me on."

"Oh Clive," I whispered. "You always feel so... god, you feel good."

He growled as he kissed me. "That's ma girl."

*L*ike the first time we met, Clive and I sat on a plane headed to Scotland.

"I'll be right back. I need to use the pisser." He kissed me then stood and left.

"Lovely," I mumbled under my breath. A flight attendant approached, asking if we needed anything.

I thought about it for a moment then smiled. "Would you happen to have whipped cream?" She smiled and shook her head no. "Oh that's okay. Sort of an inside joke between me and my boyfriend."

The woman nodded. "Would you like some tea or coffee?"

"Oh, tea would be great. May I have sugar as well?"

The woman nodded then left my side. I thought back to when we first met on the plane... what... months ago now. I smiled to myself when he told the attendant the whipped cream was for me.

"Hmm... I'll show him," I told myself. I made a mental note to purchase a few containers of whipped cream.

He made it back to his seat and sighed. "Well, long flight ahead of us, woman. I ordered a blanket," he leaned toward me and lowered his voice. "When the other blokes fall asleep, climb on top and fuck me!"

I laughed, "Clive! You're too much."

He chuckled. "So I've heard." I shook my head and he waggled his brows.

Our flight was scheduled for eighteen hours. I had no idea if we would sleep, if Clive would try to climb on top of me... I wouldn't put it past him... or if we would just pass out.

We made our connecting flight at Dulles Airport then settled in for the long leg of it to Scotland. I placed my headphones in my ears, and so did Clive. At some point, I closed my eyes and fell asleep.

I had restless dreams; my father was in most of them. He would smile when he saw me and his lips would move. I think he was saying I love you, but I could not hear him. I reached for him and him for me, but he continued to get farther and farther away.

I felt a tear slip down my face and fall into my hair. As I opened my eyes, the early morning sunlight was shining in through the plane window. I glanced over at Clive and found him still asleep. I smiled and watched him breathe. His face was peaceful and his eyes moved under the lids. I wondered if he was dreaming of me.

Turning back to the window, I lifted the visor slightly higher and glanced outside. I could see green lands below us. We had made it. I smiled and lowered the shade fully. I sat up, grabbed my purse and unbuckled, then ever so carefully, side stepped Clive without waking or touching him.

I made my way down the walkway toward the bathroom then shut the door behind me. Looking at myself in the mirror, my hair was a disheveled mess. I laughed and shook my head. After I used the bathroom and washed my hands, I made a failed attempt to smooth down my hair. I sighed and settled on pulling it behind my ears. I brushed my teeth then put my belongings back into my purse.

When I opened the door to the bathroom, I smiled when I looked up into Clive's eyes. He chuckled and waggled his brows.

"Oh no, baby. There is not enough room for that." I grinned and went to make my way past him. He looked to his left, then his right.

"Get inside. Now, woman!" He pushed against me until we were both inside. It was like being in a cramped phone booth! I smiled and tried to keep my voice down.

"There is NOT enough room, baby! I'm leaving. Do whatever you need to do and I'll see you back out there." I reached for the door when he suddenly grabbed my hand.

"No," he told me and his voice had softened. "I'm going to have sex with ye now. Drop yer panties and get on the sink." He began removing his pants and I perked a brow.

"You're serious."

"Absolutely. Now remove yer pants or I'll do it for ye." He grinned and his eyes moved down my body, then back up again.

"I think we're wasting time, but okay." I went to remove my shorts and panties and pushed them down my legs. He firmly grabbed my waist and lifted me up on the sink. He moved my legs apart and stood in between them. He reached between us and pressed the head of his cock against me, then pushed.

"Ye are wet, love. Ye wanted this as much as I did." He kissed me then thrust hard. I gasped against his lips then moaned. "Tell me, baby, tell me."

"Oh, Clive, yes!"

He pushed into me, over and over. I could not get enough of him. I leaned back and my head rested against the wall. He suddenly grabbed my legs by the backside and pushed them up against me. Clive pulled back and pushed in harder and faster. He had filled me completely.

There was a tap on the door. "Excuse me, you need to stop and get out, now," one of the flight attendants ordered.

Clive thrust harder and faster. I yelled out his name right as he came. He panted and thrust once more.

"Fuck me, woman!" He groaned and slowly pulled out. He quickly dressed himself then assisted me in doing the same. He leaned in and kissed me on the lips.

"You need to get out now!" she ordered again.

"Hold yer panties, woman! We're done!" Clive chuckled then kissed me once more. "Ready to face the masses?"

I shrugged. "I'm hiding behind you so either way, let's do it."

He grinned. "Not if I lead ye out first!" My eyes widened and I quickly shook my head no. He laughed and kissed me. "Ahh, woman, I wouldn't do that to ye. Let's go."

After being told we could never fly with them again, that we might be fined and a lot of other threats, we finally made it off the plane and headed to gather our suitcases. When we made it outside the airport, Douglas was waiting for us by one of Clive's cars. I grinned when I saw him.

"Nice to see ye again, Miss Masters." Douglas opened the car door for me.

I approached the aging man and gave him a kiss on the cheek. "It is a pleasure, Douglas. And please, do call me Abby." I sat down in the car as Clive made his way around.

"Ahh, now don't be cheating on me with Douglas, Abby." He sat down next to me in the car and wrapped an arm around me. "Douglas is quite the ladies man." He winked at Douglas, who in turn, chuckled.

~

We arrived at Clive's home and settled inside. He took me to his bedroom with our suitcases in tow.

"I would prefer ye to unpack in here, Abby. No more sleeping across the house, unless the devil in ye comes out."

I stopped what I was doing and stood there for a moment.

"The devil, Clive?" I asked then turned to face him. "What on earth do you mean?"

"I know ye lassies have yer monthly cycle. Anything that can bleed like that and live... well, let me just say that's a lot of evil ye need to release."

I blinked and stood there for a moment. I then bent over laughing, hard. "So," I started to recover, "what you're saying is, I'm releasing my evil?"

"Aye!" He chuckled then pulled me close to him. He kissed me on my nose then winked. "I want to bed ye every day woman. I want to fill ye with my seed. I want to claim ye every fucking night that I can."

I grinned and felt my face blush. "Will you allow me to be on top?"

He chuckled. "If ye like, of course."

"What all will... umm... will you do to me?" I knew Clive was dominant. I actually enjoyed being dominated. I was so used to being the dominant one for so long, it was a nice change to be controlled... in bed, of course. I loved how he would worship my body, make love to me... hard or soft. The man was so much more than I could have ever imagined.

"Oh I think that is something ye will have to discover on ye own, woman." He winked, "However, I will tell ye, there will be rope involved. Maybe some blindfolds."

I felt my panties become wet. I bit my lip and leaned into him. "Before we progress too far, we need to discuss limits. Like hard and soft limits. Just... don't hit me with a whip or anything. I don't think I can handle that."

He growled and leaned his face down into my hair. He kissed and nibbled on my neck before speaking again. "Ye might be surprised what ye would be into, love." His hand cupped my face and he kissed me softly. "Now," he kissed me once more then released me. He took a step back and placed his hands on his hips. "There is just one more conversation we need to have."

"Oh?" I asked and crossed the room to the bed. I sat down and crossed my legs. I squeezed them together in an effort to calm the fire he'd started between them.

He nodded and then crossed his arms over his chest. His arms were strong, but like this, they looked massive. Good god, Clive was hot... and he was mine!

"So since ye will be staying with me for a while... if not indefinitely," he winked and I smiled, "there's one thing we need to discuss."

I nodded and waited for what he had to say. I felt a little nervous. He had his business and the bar. I had the money my father left me. I knew I wanted to start up a non-profit organization to help those that needed assistance. I knew he could help me with this. This was a conversation we soon needed to have.

"Abby," he started. I noticed, right then, how nervous Clive looked. My brows rose and I wanted to stand, but my inner voice told me to stay seated. He sighed and lowered his gaze.

"Clive," I started, "whatever it is, just tell me." My voice was soft, but reassuring.

He nodded then turned to face me. He stepped closer until he was right in front of me. He dropped to both knees and placed his arms on either side of my hips. I wondered, for a brief second, if he was making a barricade to keep me from escaping.

Oh shit, what if he was? What if he was going to say something I didn't want to hear? His words came back just then, *So what? They're not married.* What if he was going to tell me he wanted an open relationship? I swallowed hard and waited in agony... for what was feeling like forever.

"I love ye, woman. I love ye."

My mouth dropped open. My mind was fucking me hard and I was expecting the worst, but not this. I blinked. In the past, this is when I would cut and run. I would not hang around once my target had been acquired. Once the chase was over, I bolted.

"Abby?" Clive questioned my name and kept my gaze. "Abby, yer making me nervous. Say something."

I closed my mouth and continued to stare at him. "Clive," I started then sighed.

"Oh, fuck me," he started and sat back on his heels. "Outstanding." He lowered his gaze and shook his head.

"Would you stop? I haven't even answered you yet!"

Clive lifted his gaze to mine and there was a fire there. He had opened his heart to me, even knowing all the bullshit it came with. I was damaged goods. I had no family left, well, none I would gladly claim. This man loved me, warts and all.

I smiled then reached for him. "I love you, too."

He immediately lunged for me and pulled me into a fierce hug. "Fuck woman, ye scared me!" He chuckled then kissed me.

"You are the first person I have ever said those words to," I told him, and it was the truth.

"Ahh," he started, "well that makes sense."

I furrowed my brows. "Why does that make sense?"

He shrugged. "With everything that has happened over the last few months, yer past and yer family... well, I can see how it would be hard for ye to ever tell anyone ye loved them. I understand how trust would be hard."

I nodded. This man understood me more than I had given him credit for. Hell, he understood me more than I understood myself. "The one person I should have been able to rely on, the one to have my back, completely turned on me." My gaze dropped to the floor and I sighed. "I'll only have the memory of my father when I was younger, before he... well, before he allowed work and a certain secretary to take his attentions away."

His fingers gently traced the outline of my jawline. Clive offered a hint of a smile, then he leaned in and kissed me softly. "Ye don't have to worry about anything like that again, woman. Not while ye are with me."

I nodded and reached for his hands. I held onto them a little tight, afraid if I let go, I would lose him.

"I'm not going anywhere, Abby."

I met his gaze and smiled. "I love you, Clive Patterson."

He chuckled. "I love ye, Abby Masters."

ime passed quickly after we arrived in Scotland. It still seemed surreal that my father died. I'm still not sure how I feel about it, regardless if it was permanent. I can say I have not accepted he is gone... yet... but truth be told, it does not feel like anything has changed. I never saw him, we never talked, and he was seldom home.

As for the woman who was my mother, she left the house once handcuffs were placed on her and she was escorted out. The police informed me she was acting like a squatter and refused to leave the house. A pair of handcuffs and a booking in the city jail later, they held her for the upcoming trial for the murder of my father. Lexi has emailed me and let me know she's trying to find me. I wrote her back with *tough shit. She should have thought of that before she tried condemning me to hell.*

Mail arrived today and with it, a package from Makayla. She must have been on duty to empty my PO Box. I'm grateful the three of us patched things between us. I have missed them terribly. Hell, I miss them now.

I pulled the strip off the large manila envelope and found a few items inside: a letter from my attorney, a few bills, information from my bank and a letter without a return address.

"Who would do that?" I asked myself. Clive walked into the room about that time and wrapped his arms around my waist, then kissed my neck. He asked me to stay with him permanently. This new adventure of being involved with someone because I choose to be is different. There have been times I found myself shrinking away from him, but as soon as I did, he would come after me. He has made sure to remind me how much he loves and needs me.

This made me happy, but sometimes, it is not enough. I need to be happy with myself and the decision to share my life with someone. My fear is bringing him into the hell that is my world. What does he say to this? BRING IT ON! He will usually follow it up with what I call a man titty grunt. He grunts hard, flexes, and holds his arms out front. The first time he did this, I almost fell over laughing.

I turned my face toward him and kissed him softly. He smiled then patted my behind.

"What came for ye, love?" He asked and plopped down on the sofa.

"Something from my attorney, bills, and an anonymous envelope," I told him.

"Ooh, secret agent Abby!" He chuckled and I shook my head.

I opened the letter from my attorney first.

Dear Miss Masters,

Your father's assets have been settled and formally transitioned into your name. The home has been signed over to the state, as you requested. A few bids have already been placed on it and there's a possibility it will go to a foster orphanage.

I've included a few legal documents you will need to sign and return to me at your earliest convenience. I had my paralegal highlight the areas so there is no confusion.

If there is anything you need, please do not hesitate to ask. I enjoyed
working for your father and will continue to be of service to you.
Thank you and regards,
Thomas Billings
Billings and Ascrew, Attorneys at Law

"As long as I knew my attorney, I had no idea what his name actually was. His name is Thomas Billings?" I glanced over at Clive, who simply shrugged. I set the letter down then turned the anonymous envelope over and slid my finger through the top, opening it up.

I skipped to the bottom for the signature, curious to who would not offer a return address. My eyes widened a little and my lips parted.

"Blaine?"

"Who, love?" Clive stood and looked over my shoulder. His hands rested on my shoulders, but I did not answer him. I stared at the signature for a few minutes.

Blaine took so much of me... and I allowed him to. For so long I wanted him to want me, but he didn't. He wanted his music and his drugs. Last time I heard from him, he had cleaned up and actually attempted an apology.

"Fucking asshole," I mumbled and set the letter down. I did not want to read anything he had to say. I pulled away from Clive and crossed the den to the windows. Pulling the curtain to the side, I looked outside across the lawn. The sun was beginning to set, not that it mattered. I was not actually looking at anything.

Seeing his name brought up memories that I had been trying to forget, memories that I want to put behind me. I crossed my arms over my chest in an effort to hold myself together. As soon as you feel everything is coming together, something explodes... like a grenade, and blows it apart.

"Ye should read this, love," Clive announced.

"Why? So I can relive how much of a shit hole I was to my friends?"

"Shit hole? Is that even possible?"

I turned and glared at him, but could not stay mad long. The look on his face, the look of confusion, made me smile. What happened with Blaine was not Clive's fault. I lowered my gaze and crossed the room to him. I sighed and looked up. "I'm sorry."

He smiled and kissed me softly. "Nothing to be sorry about. Ye should read it though, woman." He smiled softly and handed it over. "I'll give ye a minute. Call for me when ye are ready."

I nodded and he kissed me once more. "I love ye," he whispered.

"I love you." I watched him as he left the room. It was so quiet. I could hear my pulse in my ears.

Taking in a deep breath, I slowly exhaled, then pulled Blaine's letter into view.

Abby,

I heard about your father. Telling you I'm sorry this way is just wrong. I don't know how to get ahold of you so please forgive me.

When I heard, I immediately tried to call, but the line was changed. Please know you'll be in my thoughts. I've included tour information so if I'm ever in your area, please come out and see us. Call my manager, Chuck, and he'll get you hooked up.

Take care and please know, I regret every day how I treated you and Lexi. If I could take it all back, I would.

Sincerely,

Blaine

I swiped a tear from my eye that tried to escape. I set the letter down and cleared my throat. "You may come back now, Clive." He peeked around the corner with raised brows. I smiled. "You did not have to leave."

"Aye, I know, but ye needed the time to read it." He came closer and pulled me into a hug. "What do ye think ye would like to do while making residence in Scotland?"

I shrugged. "I want to look into helping people who are transitioning from abusive relationships and situations. I want to help them, to let them know there is life outside of it."

He smiled. "I think that would be great, love." He kissed me. "Aye, healing is good for the soul." He winked.

I couldn't agree more.

~

I had been seeing a counselor for a few months since I left Texas. He has helped me in many ways, and in some instances, I had already improved more than anticipated. The yoga and meditation helped tremendously.

Clive teased me he would do yoga just to watch me bend over in downward facing dog. I teased back that I was doing this to practice for the bedroom. His mouth dropped open and I giggled.

Tonight, we were celebrating us, moving forward, and wine. Yes, lots and lots of wine needed to be celebrated.

Scarlet saw me when I walked inside and she squealed. "ABBY!" She immediately pulled me into a hug and squeezed... hard.

"Scarlet... breathe... help..." She released me and I smiled. "I was teasing!"

She shook her finger to me then smiled. "Well? How do ye feel being a Scotsman now?"

I glanced down my body, then back to her. I flipped my hands over as if to inspect them. "Last time I checked, Scarlet, I'm not a Scotsman."

"Well, Scotswoman?"

I shook my head. "I'm still American. I have not given up my status." I leaned in and lowered my voice. "Clive and I are not married, either."

"Yet," she winked.

"What?" I pulled back and blinked a few times in surprise. "Did he say something about marriage? Because if he did, oh Scarlet, I'm not ready! He can't marry me! Oh shit..."

"Oy!" She yelled at me then grabbed my arms. "Shut it, would ye? He's not said anything about it yet, Abby. Calm the fuck down!"

"Oh," now I felt foolish. "I'm sorry." I pulled her hands off my arms and took a step back. The thought of Clive asking me to marry him... well that set off alarms. Alarms that show I'm not ready for that type of commitment yet.

Why not? You moved here to be with him. Marriage is only a contract.

And vows.

A contract with vows. Semantics.

Oh shut up!

"Abby?" Scarlet brought me back from my mental argument. "What if he did ask you to marry him?"

I sat down in a chair close to me. The bar was busy and the noise level was quite loud. Considering the thought of marriage brought on a headache... or maybe it was the noise level.

I loved him so much. He'd done so much for me, more than I would have ever done for anyone else. He saw me when no one else did. He loves me, no matter what I have done or how I have fucked up. He saw me at my worst when my father died and my mother shit on me... and he's still here. He opened his home to me... all this without asking for anything in return.

Would I marry this man?

Yes, yes I would.

I smiled and met Scarlet's stare. I nodded with a smile. She squealed again and clapped her hands.

"OY!" A familiar male voice yelled over the crowd. The crowd quieted down and everyone looked toward the bar. The man who spoke made his way on top of the bar. He looked over and smiled, then winked at me. Damn he looked good in his fitted black t-shirt and kilt. His hair was styled just so. He began to wave me over.

People in the pub turned toward me and formed an open line toward the bar. I looked at Scarlet, who shrugged, then back at the man. He smiled that sexy smile of his and waved once again.

"Aye! Abby, get up here!"

I grinned and made my way toward the bar. A few hands took mine and helped me up by way of lifting me. I suddenly felt like Jennifer Grey from *Dirty Dancing*.

Clive took my hand, pulled it to his lips, and kissed the back of it. "I love ye, woman," he said just to me. I smiled and blushed slightly.

"I love you, too."

"All right!" He turned back toward the crowd. "This here is ma lady! Her name is Abby and that's all you need to know. Oh and I'm fucking her!"

I gasped and turned on him. Woots and hollers rang out as did clapping and "get her!"

"I cannot believe you just said that!" I was shocked, but also amused. No one has ever announced their love for me to a crowd by way of saying, "I'm fucking her."

He chuckled. "What, love? Would you rather I tell them we're getting married?"

I took a step back. Clive must have read the shock on my face because he quickly grabbed a hold of me.

"Don't worry, love, I would not do that to ye," he winked, "promise."

I nodded and smiled. I then turned back to the crowd and cleared my throat. "HEY!" I was surprised how loud my voice rang out. I felt Clive lean over a little and he chuckled softly.

"Ye might have a little Scot in ye yet," he told me.

I grinned and gave him a sly look. "No, but I will later."

He grinned and patted my behind. "That's ma girl."

I turned back to the audience, whose attention I gained. "So all y'all know I'm a southern girl from Texas. I'm not Scottish. Something else you also need to know," I pursed my lips and felt my face immediately blush with what I was about to announce. "I'm fucking him, too!"

It was quiet for a second, then chaos broke out. Cheers, clapping, woots, and whistling rang throughout the bar. I laughed and Clive pulled me close to him. He kissed me... long and hard. He bent me back slightly and held onto my frame. My arms wrapped around his neck. His tongue slipped over my lips as he invaded my mouth. I whimpered softly and pulled him closer.

"GET A ROOM!" Scarlet yelled out and she received a few laughs. Clive finally, reluctantly, released me. He kissed me once more then jumped off the bar. He took me by the waist and helped me down.

"I am going to hurt ye later tonight, woman! Oh, I'm so going to hurt ye!"

I grinned and shook my head. "You have to catch me first!" I quickly sidestepped Clive and ran out from behind the bar. He reached for me and barely missed. He shook his finger at me then made a mock gesture of a spanking.

I laughed and went back to Scarlet. I took a seat again and a few people I recognized from the bar congratulated me. Scarlet took a seat and smiled so big, I thought it was going to break her face.

"I'm SO excited for ye, Abby!" She sighed and glanced across the crowd. "I wish Jacob would do something like that for me. Well, then again, maybe not. That was right embarrassing!" She laughed.

I giggled then nodded. "Just a little, but it will always be memorable."

EPILOGUE

I've been in Scotland for three years now. I've been in therapy for what has been called "daddy issues." Clive has been supportive and suggested it early on. I had nightmares sometimes. Sometimes I was looking into the burial site where my father was laid to rest. The coffin would open up and he would reach for me, begging me to save him. Other times it was my mother, drunk, and trying to set our house on fire with me in it.

I would wake up screaming. Clive was always there. He would hold me, tell me it was okay. In time, he finally brought up the idea of talking with someone.

While my time in India was great, it helped me in ways therapy could not. I learned how to center myself, learned how to meditate and push out the negative that was happening around me.

This was not so effective while I dreamed, though. I was reluctant to start anything that had to do with talking about my feelings.

The first few sessions I barely said anything. I then began

opening up a little more. Six sessions in, the therapist suggested bringing Clive into it. He agreed and joined me.

We've been attending the sessions together now for almost two years. The therapist has given what he called a clean bill of health. I doubt he'll ever be able to cure my nightmares, but one day, maybe they'll stop coming.

Today was a special day. Clive and I were celebrating our three-year anniversary together. He asked me to dress up, so I did. Scarlet went shopping with me at the local mall in town. I picked up a red dress made of satin material. It clung to my body and the hem ended above my knees. It was sleeveless and the top plunged deep, giving a great view of my breasts.

I knew Clive would love this dress.

"He would most likely love it on the floor, Abby," Scarlet informed me with a giggle.

"Most likely, yes," I told her.

I set my hair in ringlets and allowed them to cascade down my back. My make-up was darker than normal to accompany the evening shade. I applied a dark red lipstick to my lips, followed by a shimmer gloss. I wore the diamond earrings he gave me last year for our two-year anniversary.

Placing my black stiletto heels on my feet, I was ready to go. The sound of my walk echoed down the hallway as I left our bedroom and headed toward the den. I leaned against the wall, one arm up on the door jam. I placed my other hand on my hip then cleared my throat.

Clive turned to face me in his dark grey suit top and accompanying kilt. He'd styled his hair perfectly. He smirked and a single brow rose. "Damn, woman! Look at ye." He ran a hand down his freshly shaved face then closed the distance between us. "Hell, we are staying in tonight. Get in the room! I'm making love to ye, woman, right now! Ye got me all hard!"

I glanced down and saw the man was speaking the truth. He was hard under his kilt. I slowly moved my eyes back up his body then stepped closer. I leaned against him and rested my palms on his chest.

"No, I want to go out. You can then take my dress off with your teeth, if you so like." I winked then kissed him softly on his lips.

He growled then followed it with, "Fuck, woman."

Eventually, we made it out to one of our cars. Douglas drove us over to Castle Terrace restaurant. Later, Clive promised to take me to the Fudge House bakery. He raved about their exquisite desserts and I've put off going there as long as possible. Why? Who knows, but I honestly could not wait to try them.

Clive leaned in and whispered, "Ye look beautiful tonight, ma lady." His arm was around my shoulders and he squeezed me closer.

I smiled and squeezed his thigh. "You are definitely getting some tonight, baby." He grinned then chuckled softly. He kissed the side of my head and continued to whisper in my ear the many things he was planning for me tonight at home. My hand squeezed his thigh a little more, then inched closer between his legs. I touched him softly and gently stroked his head. He growled a few times in my ear, which in turn, made me wet.

We arrived, just in time, as Clive was beginning to fondle me under my dress. "Ye are not wearing panties? Fuck..." he trailed off and stared at me.

"Well, neither are you."

"Woman, I do not wear panties."

I absolutely laughed out loud at this. "That is not what I meant and you know it!" He laughed along with me.

"That's ma girl," he whispered, just as Douglas opened my door.

Clive tried the best he could to adjust himself in his kilt. He finally gave up and went with the evident hard on underneath his clothes. I tried not to giggle... too much.

We were seated in a corner of the restaurant and the

atmosphere was busy, but surprisingly quiet. We had our dinner, me a chicken breast with sweet potato and him, Orange Birch Bolete. I was still becoming accustomed to Scottish foods, which seemed to be mostly seafood.

The food was delicious, some of the best I have had in a long time. We sipped some of the wine, produced by Patterson Distillery, then followed up dinner with coffee.

"I love ye, woman," Clive told me. He reached across the table and rubbed his thumb lightly on my palm.

"I love you, too, baby."

"I need to ask ye something." He pulled his hand away and fished for something in the breast pocket of his jacket.

I picked up my napkin and dabbed the corners of my mouth. I sat it down then crossed my legs.

"I have loved every moment of being with ye, as ye well know." I smiled at this. I could not imagine what it would have been like for me, to be in his position. Would I have stayed with someone who had as many issues as I did? For the love of this man, absolutely I would have.

"I have loved it as well," I told him.

"Good." He cleared his throat then sighed. He rose to his feet and came closer toward me. Clive took in a deep breath then lowered down to one knee.

My eyes immediately widened and my heart pounded in my ears. Oh my god... is he doing this? Is he really doing this now? His lips were moving, but I could not hear anything. Shit! What was he saying?

I closed my eyes and looked away from him. I grabbed my wine and took a sip, then changed my mind and drank the glass. I sat it down then cleared my throat. Once I let out the breath I had been holding, I turned back to face him.

"Right," he started, then nodded with a smile. "Take two?" I smiled and offered a reassuring smile. "Abby, ye came into ma life when I least expected it. Ye brought so much love and laughter. I find maself thinking of ye, wanting to know what ye are doing, where ye are, who ye are with... just so I can hear ye voice."

"Oh, Clive," I started.

He shook his head and took my hand. "Our lives have only just begun, woman. I want to share mine with ye, forever, if ye will have me. Will ye marry me, ma beautiful Abby?"

My vision blurred slightly due to the tears that had formed. I squeezed his hand and felt myself nod. "Yes!" I screamed, "YES!"

Clive quickly scooped me up from my chair and hugged me tightly against him. People around us clapped. He released me then slid a beautiful diamond ring onto my finger. It was round in shape and looked to be two carats. The setting appeared to be almost antique.

"Clive, oh my god. It is so beautiful!"

"It was ma mother's," he told me. "She gave it to me, just before she died."

I looked into his eyes and smiled. "Thank you so much! I love it. I wish I could tell her the same." I pulled him to me and kissed him, hard. After paying our bill, we left the restaurant and headed toward home. Dessert would have to wait for another night. I wanted my fiancé tonight, and he wanted me. Then, with the thought of fiancé, I paused.

"Clive, who will walk me down the aisle?" I had not considered this before now. I had written off ever getting married... until I met Clive.

"Who would you want to give you away?" He asked me, then kissed me softly as we pulled up to the house.

"I don't know. I mean," he took my hand and helped me out of the car. He slipped his arm around my waist and pulled me close as we entered the house. "I plan to tell my friends so they can come out. I may walk alone, or maybe have Lexi or Makayla do it."

"Ahh, now see? Wedding plans in the works already." He grinned and closed the bedroom door, hell bent on getting me out of my dress. I wanted to make love to my soon to be husband tonight… and every night the rest of our lives together.

~

*T*he day had finally arrived. I wore a halter-style wedding gown that was a cream ivory satin finish. The waist had lace hugging my sides, from under my arms, down to my hips. The front was cut to the mid-calf where the backside trailed behind me.

I decided on a small veil that hung down behind my hair. The lower part of my hair was pinned in small ringlets to my head. The rest was pulled to the side and braided, then finished just above the pinned curls. My make-up was perfect.

I stood staring in the mirror to my reflection and smiled. The light pink lipstick I wore was subtle, as was the smoky eye make-up.

Douglas appeared in the reflection behind me. He looked proud, as if looking at his own daughter. I turned to face him and held my arms out.

"So, good?"

He shook his head. "No, perfect, ma dear. Absolutely perfect." He stepped closer, "If yer ready, Mr. Patterson is ready."

I smiled. "How does he look?"

"Oh, he's hot all right," Scarlet grinned.

I glanced over at her with a grin. "Excellent. Now," I turned back to Douglas, "I do believe I'm ready."

"Then it would be ma honor, ma lady." He held out his elbow for me and I slipped my hand into the crook of it.

After Clive asked for my hand in marriage, I discussed with him the possibility of having Douglas walk me down the aisle. He loved the idea. When I approached Douglas about it, I believe that was the first time I'd seen the man shed a tear.

"I would be absolutely honored, ma lady."

The doors to the church were closed and Douglas stood with me, ready to walk me to my future husband. My ladies, Lexi and Makayla, were in place and ready to walk down the aisle first.

The doors opened and Scarlet took the lead, followed by Makayla then Lexi. The doors closed and I took one final deep breath, then glanced over at Douglas. He smiled and offered a nod, which I returned.

The music shifted to the wedding march and the doors opened once again. Everyone in the church stood and smiled. I gripped Douglas' arm a little tighter.

"Easy does it, ma lady. I have you, I promise."

I exhaled and smiled as I caught Clive's gaze. He stood with his traditional Scottish clothing and kilt. The man looked like he stepped off a runway magazine into the church. I swooned over my fiancé right then.

Douglas led me to Clive and handed me over to him. I took his hands and turned to face him. The minister went through the ceremony rather quickly; he didn't waste any time. When it came to our vows, I felt a little nervous. Clive went first.

"I have never, in ma life, met anyone like ye, Abby. Ye have managed to turn everything I knew upside down, in the best way possible. I cannot imagine another single day without ye by ma side, woman. Ye are everything I could hope to find in a woman, and more. I love ye and love everything about ye. Possibilities are endless with ye on ma arm," he lowered his voice just for me, "hell, in ma bed!" He grinned and I blushed. "Ye are making me the happiest man alive today by becoming ma wife. I love ye, Abby. I love ye so much."

Clive leaned in and kissed me softly. The minister chuckled and interrupted us. "I've not announced for ye to kiss her yet."

"Aye, but she's mine, regardless."

I grinned and looked at the minister. He offered me a nod and I inhaled deeply. Slowly, I exhaled and began my own vows.

"Clive, my sweet, handsome devil, Clive. I had no idea I'd met my future husband on the plane that day in Texas. You caught me off guard and completely plunged into my life. I watch you, how you are with people and honestly, you make me want to be a better person. I love you so much. You were there for me at the worst time of my life and never faltered. Now, I wish to return the favor and be your wife and be there for you. I will always be by your side, no matter what. You saw me when no one else did. I will always be yours. Always. I love you, Clive Patterson. Always. I cannot wait to be your wife, experience my new life as a Scottish woman, and give you little Scottish babies." Clive chuckled at this. "I love you so much."

The minister took our rings and handed mine to Clive. He slipped it on my finger. "With this ring, I thee wed."

I slipped his onto his finger. "With this ring, I thee wed."

The minister smiled and placed a hand on our shoulders. "What the world brought together, let no man tear asunder. I now pronounce you, husband and wife." He grinned between us. "You may now snog yer wife!"

I laughed and Clive grinned. He growled softly and pulled me close, then kissed me with everything he had.

The church roared in approvals with clapping and cheers. When our kiss ended, I glanced at my girls, who were all smiles. Lexi dabbed her eyes and Makayla offered a small fist pump in the air.

Clive hugged me close and I looked up into his eyes. "I love you, Mr. Patterson."

He grinned. "I love you, too, Mrs. Patterson."

THE END

Continue the Southern Roots series with the next story, Driven Hunger!
Here's Chapter One

*S*ummer was just beginning and with it, a fresh start. She moved into an apartment after her breakup with Conner and had never felt happier. Having the distance and serenity of being alone, away from him, opened her eyes to new possibilities.

Makayla had enrolled in the University of Texas at Arlington after their break up to complete her degree in social work. Eventually, she wanted to earn her degree in psychology. Since she was a young girl, she'd known she wanted to help people. She completed an internship after her graduation from college and had since joined a practice as a social worker.

She slipped the mailbox key in the slot and turned it. After opening the metal door, she found a few pieces of mail that were addressed to Abby. She flipped through them quickly until one from Deep Ember Productions caught her attention.

She turned it over and ran her finger underneath the seal.

"If anything comes from Blaine, just keep it. I plan on staying here in Scotland; there's nothing he has that I want," Abby had told her just before she made the final decision to move to Scotland.

After Abby's father died, she'd packed up her belongings, put the family home and estate up for sale, and moved to Scotland. She was now married to Clive and happiness suited her. Makayla was thrilled for her friend.

She pulled out the typed note.

Abby,

If you can make it out to one of our shows, I've included private passes. The crew would enjoy seeing you, and so would I.

Your terms. I'm trying to right my wrongs, one step at a time. If you accept, give my manager, Chuck, a call. He'll set you up at the hotel, and with the passes for you and any of your friends.

Regards,

Blaine

Makayla glanced into the envelope and found a business card that said *Chuck Bradshaw, band and production manager* with a phone number and email.

"What does he expect Abby to do? Drop and run to him?" She shook her head and shoved the letter and card back into the envelope. "Asshat."

After locking the mailbox and turning toward the post office door, she considered the possibility of a concert, seeing Blaine and his crew…a girl's night out.

"As much as I can't stand that damn prick, it would be fun to go party with them. The rest of 'em weren't so bad, just that asshole who thinks he's God's gift to…hell, whatever." She huffed and fiddled with her keys until the car key was in hand. "He's right up there with Conner."

She unlocked her truck and climbed inside. Turning it on, she grabbed the vanity mirror and opened it. Her long brown hair had been straightened this morning with her flat iron, but the humidity decided frizzed ends would be more appropriate. She rolled her eyes and dabbed at the excess eyeliner that tended to run with the humidity.

"I fucking hate Texas sometimes."

She flipped the vanity up and glanced over at her phone. She could call now and make the plans, or she could trash the letter. She sighed and turned her phone over in her purse, placing it face down.

Blaine's letter stuck out the top of her purse, and she casually pulled it out again. She studied the note inside, not necessarily paying attention to the letter itself. Her fingers slipped over the letters then she paused. Without thinking of her actions, she decided a concert was what she needed; even if it was with one of the worst people in the world: Blaine.

Makayla dialed the number on the business card. Her heart picked up rhythm and she felt her chest tighten. Taking a step to put herself into her self-proclaimed "enemy's" territory was not something Makayla did often...if ever. She was not a fighter and never wanted to fight with Conner, but she'd had no choice most nights. If someone else was involved, she never backed down from a fight, but she didn't make a habit of walking into one.

The phone rang once and picked up. Makayla's throat tightened again but instead of a voice answering, voicemail picked up. She sighed a hard, heavy sigh and waited for the message to complete.

"You've reached Chuck Bradshaw. Leave a message and depending on the urgency, I'll get back to you."

The message ended and the phone beeped for her to begin talking.

"Umm, hello... my name is Makayla Shaw. I'm friends with Abby Masters. Blaine sent her ticket information and she handed it off to me. I was hoping to get said tickets for the next event here in Texas." She left her number and hung up the phone.

"I highly doubt I'll hear back, but maybe because it was sent to Abby..." her thoughts trailed off as she put her phone down and put her truck into gear. "Whatever."

A short drive later, she pulled up to the carport to her apartment complex. The apartment did not have a garage, but this was just as good.

Makayla glanced at the empty spot in the driveway next to her. Her heart felt heavy tonight, she would love to share her home with someone. Pulling the keys from the ignition, she made her way up the sidewalk to the staircase of her apartment building. She opened her door and walked inside to a dark living room. The smell of cinnamon filled the air from the incense around her house.

"I love the smell of Christmas, no matter what time of the year it is," she told Conner once upon a time.

"That is the craziest shit I've heard from you, woman," Conner replied. *"What if I like the smell of...Easter?"*

"Easter? Easter doesn't have a smell, doofus."

"Yes it does," he told her with a frown. *"Chocolate and chicken shit."*

She raised a brow, *"Oh God, Conner, seriously? Chicken shit?"*

"Yeah and if you keep eating the chocolate, your ass will get too big for your pants. They are almost splitting at the seams now."

Makayla shook off the memory and stared at the air freshener in the wall. Her vision blurred slightly. "Fuck, I'm NOT crying over him anymore! I need a drink." She flipped a few lights on and the tan walls came into view. She'd wanted a rustic look to her home and that's what she'd made for herself, complete with small versions of wagon wheels made of wood on the walls. She loved rustic anything and planned to decorate her home accordingly.

The kitchen was a reflection of her imagination. The fridge was stainless steel and had cute magnets on it of different cactus, western boots, and stars. She pulled the door open and reached in for a Shiner Bock beer. She enjoyed the German beer and it didn't matter to her that it was produced in Texas. It was good.

The cool liquid chilled her throat as she took a long pull. She set it on the counter and pulled out the leftovers from last night, cold pizza.

"Living single has its perks. I don't have to cook often and there's no one here to tell me when I should be home, no one to tell where I'm going and definitely no one to tell me I shouldn't eat an entire batch of brownies I just made. Fuck'em and their seams." She took another pull of her beer then grabbed the pizza.

She made her way into the den and sat down on the couch. She turned on the television and began watching the local news.

After ingesting two slices of cold pizza, followed by three beers, Makayla was feeling better...and maybe a little buzzed. She was watching the television but not paying attention to what was being said.

Then her phone rang. She didn't care to answer it. *Whoever it is can leave a damn message*, she thought to herself.

Her home voicemail carried her voice through the den. When it beeped, she half listened to whoever may be calling.

"Yes, Makayla, this is Chuck Bradshaw's assistant. I'm calling to let you know tickets will be provided to you and ten of your friends, including private passes. Blaine requested to have you personally escorted to their green room once you arrive."

Makayla coughed on her beer when she heard this. The message continued to play and she sat there, staring at the floor.

"Blaine wants to see me? Oh, this can't be good," she told herself. "Last time I saw him...wow, when I found him and Abby fucking in the bathroom." She shook her head and closed her eyes. The way Blaine had stared at her, the violence in his demeanor... there's no way she'd feel comfortable being in the same room with him, sober or not. She sighed and lowered her head. "Shit, I need another beer."

~

A few days after the call from Chuck Bradshaw's assistant, the tickets arrived by way of registered mail, along with extra tickets and private passes, and one pass for the green room as promised. Makayla sighed and sat the envelope on her table.

"Well, here's to moving forward, I suppose. As much as I don't like the idea of being alone with Blaine, I'm going. Besides," she righted herself and squared her shoulders, "he doesn't scare me. Hell, I'll kick his ass if it's needed."

She smirked at her own thoughts and considered the other band members. She remembered them all, especially Matt. He had replaced their old drummer just before Deep Ember made it big.

Matt had a sweet smile, beautiful eyes, and a great personality.

He also didn't put up with Blaine's shit. Even more reason to like him.

"Maybe seeing the band won't be so bad after all," she told herself.

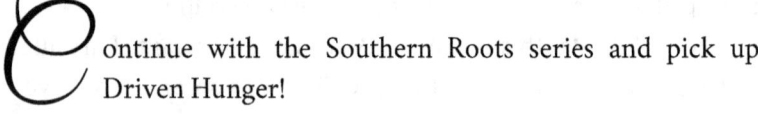ontinue with the Southern Roots series and pick up Driven Hunger!

Check out Misadventures with a Firefighter, available now!

Misadventures of a Firefighter

Cara Murphy is a New York City kindergarten teacher with a bright future and tenure on the horizon, and she won't let anything—any man—distract her. She's had her heart broken before, and she won't make that mistake twice. She's got her career to focus on, and being single has many, many advantages.

Noah Hughes is a firefighter with a charred heart who heats up every room he enters, but he lives solely for the happiness of his five-year-old son. When he crosses paths with Cara at a club, sparks fly, and they share a hot night of passion. But that flame is quickly doused during a surprise second encounter.

Continuing to see each other would truly be playing with fire, but Cara and Noah can't stop. Still, Cara's career is in jeopardy, and Noah's heart is locked in guilt. Is there really a chance they could build a love that forever burns bright?

Preorder

Misadventures with a Lawyer

Legendary lawyer Chase Newstrom is as famous in court as he is with the ladies. His work-hard, play-harder mindset is why he's never lost a case...or lacked a model on his arm. But a recent twist before the bench threatens to derail his perfect record.

Chase turns to junior associate Ainsley Speire to solve his case's problems after hours so he can gallivant around town with yet another lady friend, and Ainsley, despite being driven and focused, is none too pleased with her boss's demands. She's had to cancel long-standing plans at the last minute, again...and vows it's for the last time.

Ainsley sits down with Chase's most expensive scotch in one hand and fancy pen in the other and pours it all out, literally and figuratively. When Chase finds the note—and a passed-out Ainsley—he's intrigued. Perhaps there's more to the soft-spoken Ms. Speire than he thought.

Ainsley wakes to Chase's trademark cocky grin, and Chase sees a new spark in Ainsley's eyes. Anything between them would be an HR nightmare, but is there a chance Chase and Ainsley are willing to work together on one more case? A case that promises a lifetime sentence of love?

Read these stories in KU!

Southern Roots series

Southern Roots

City Lights

Fueled Desire

Driven Hunger

Paramour

Playing Her Body

Suspenseful Seduction World

Submitting to Paradise

Claiming His Snow

Hot SEALs

Guarded by a SEAL

Available wide!

Special Ops series

Delta Force

Sniper

Misadventures series

Misadventures with a Firefighter

Misadventures with a Lawyer

ABOUT THE AUTHOR

USA TODAY and Award-winning Bestselling Author, Julie Morgan (writing as J. Morgan), holds a degree in Computer Science and loves science fiction shows and movies. Encouraged by her family, she began writing. Originally from Texas, Julie now resides in Central Florida with her husband and daughter where she is an advocate for Special Needs children and can be found playing games with her daughter when she isn't lost in another world.

Keep up with Julie. Join her newsletter and receive a free book!
www.juliemorganbooks.com/newsletter.html
julie@juliemorganbooks.com

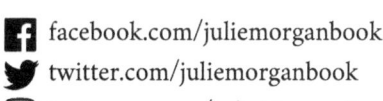

facebook.com/juliemorganbook
twitter.com/juliemorganbook
instagram.com/JulieMorganBooks

www.ingramcontent.com/pod-product-compliance
Lightning Source LLC
Chambersburg PA
CBHW060934180626
46817CB00004B/1543